T0148344

RE-MEDITATIONS

DESCARTES VINDICATED

FREDERICK BAUER

IUNIVERSE, INC.
NEW YORK   BLOOMINGTON

Re-Meditations
Descartes Vindicated

iUniverse books may be ordered through booksellers or by contacting:

iUniverse
1663 Liberty Drive
Bloomington, IN 47403
www.iuniverse.com
1-800-Authors (1-800-288-4677)

*Because of the dynamic nature of the Internet, any Web addresses or links
contained in this book may have changed since publication and may no longer
be valid.*

ISBN: 978-1-4401-6737-9 (sc)
ISBN: 978-1-4401-6738-6 (ebk)

Printed in the United States of America

iUniverse rev. date: 8/13/2009

CONTENTS

Thanks, Charles, for the suggestion.

FORWORD

A warning. What you will learn as you read this book may utterly change what you believe about the world and, more than that, what you believe about yourself.

Before you read what follows, then, take a moment to mull over the following question. What would you say is harder to believe: i) that 500,000 atoms stacked, one on top of another, would make a pile no higher than this piece of paper is thick, or ii) that what you see right now is not a piece of paper, not a page in a book, but part of a movie-like visual field of colors in your mind?

To take in the full impact of the first item, the half-million-atom pile no higher than this page is thick, look at the page from its edge and ask if that can possibly be true.* As you think about it, consider what the author of *Explaining the Atom* wrote: "200, 000, 000 hydrogen atoms could be placed one next to the other in an inch." That's four hundred times a half-million. And most of the half-million-atom pile will be almost entirely empty space! (*A majority of my students last semester said "Not possible"!)

As for the second item, consider this. It was discovered long before anyone had even the faintest notion that the true facts about physical bodies are nearly incomprehensible, and certainly almost unbelievable. What you see is something entirely private to you. Take a moment to realize that what appears to be this page is not the only thing you see right now. Stare at this X and, while you're doing it, notice that your field of vision extends from an edge at your right to an edge at your left, from the edge above the X to the edge below it. (The edges are what "peripheral vision" refers to.) That means that you don't see just the color of what seems to be the page, but the colors of all the other items in your total visual field. Think of it as a movie. What you see when you are watching a movie or a television program is a large picture with many colors. That will help you understand what is meant by saying that your total visual field is like a movie. When you run your eyes around the room you're sitting in, your eyes are like cameras scanning an entire scene. But the colors exist only in your mind. If there are things outside your mind, the screen of patterned colors will block you from seeing them. What's more, the colors 'go poof' as soon as you close your eyes.

Most people, even physicists who believe the claim about atoms, want no part of this second fact. Nevertheless, both of those facts are true. Or, if not both, then at least the fact about what you see. To learn why, you must discover for yourself what René Descartes discovered in the first half of the 1600's.

René Descartes. Descartes is the most important thinker of modern times. The reason is quite simple. He brought together the two most important threads of modern physics and physiology, that is, two discoveries fully worthy of the title "modern-scientific," to make a monumental advance in human psychology.

The first of those two 'threads' is the theory that the only things in the world of three-dimensional bodies are infinitesimally tiny particles or collections of them. The 1500's and 1600's saw an explosion of new discoveries built on that theory, often referred to as "atomism." Although the theory had been put forward in the fifth century B. C. by the Greek thinkers, Leucippus and Democritus, it was largely ignored after the common-sense attack mounted against it by Aristotle. However, at the end of the Middle Ages, dominated by Aristotle's science, various European thinkers revived the atomists' theory. Improved by the introduction of rigorous mathematical measurement by Galileo, Descartes, Newton, and others, it became the foundation of nearly all modern thinking about physical realities. Richard Feynman, winner of a Nobel Prize in physics, thought so highly of the atomist foundation of the modern sciences that, in his famous lectures on physics, he wrote:

> If, in some cataclysm, all of scientific knowledge were to be destroyed, and only one sentence passed on to the next generation of creatures, what statement would contain the most information in the fewest words? I believe it is the atomic hypothesis (or the atomic fact, or whatever you wish to call it) that all things are made of atoms—little particles that move around in perpetual motion, attracting each other when they are a little distance apart, but repelling upon being squeezed into one another. In that one sentence, you will see, there is an enormous amount of information about the world, if just a little imagination and

thinking are applied. (R. Feynman, *The Feynman Lectures of Physics*, Vol. I, p.1-2.)

The other 'thread' is the modern discovery of the true role of the five senses. Rather than enabling us to see, hear, smell, taste, or feel rocks, squirrels, brains, or other 3-D bodies, our eyes, ears, etc., merely send nerve impulses via afferent neurons to the brain whenever they are activated by light, vibrations, and other stimuli from the environment. Sensation only provides clues to things in the environment.

By putting those discoveries together, Descartes became the most revolutionary thinker in the entire history of human thought. He showed that, instead of having direct acquaintance with the world outside our imaginations, we must use reason to interpret the clues provided by sense-input in order to learn the truth about that outside world. Stephen Pinker, a Harvard professor, summed up the conclusion that follows logically from Descartes' revolutionary advance in understanding how our senses work:

> Plato said that we are trapped inside a cave and know the world only through the shadows it casts on the wall. The skull is our cave, and mental representations are the shadows. The information in an internal representation is all that we can know about the world. (S. Pinker, *How the Mind Works*, 1997, p.84)

Instead of direct acquaintance with outside realities, therefore, we have direct acquaintance only with representations of those realities. Of course, if the things represented by the representations do not exist, then it is more accurate to call them "deceptions" than "representations.

The possibility that what we sense are not representations of reality frightens most of today's thinkers so much that, rather than praise Descartes, they revile him.

Widespread hostility to Descartes' science/ philosophy. A few years ago, Harry McFarland Bracken wrote a short work on Descartes' worldview. Here is how he introduced Chapter One:

> Although René Descartes is often called the "father of modern philosophy," he has been attacked, reviled, and condemned like no other thinker for most of the last 350 years. Even Pope John Paul II has recently felt the need to criticize him. Refutations continue to pile up. European philosophy is haunted by Descartes and his ideas. (H. Bracken, *Descartes*, 2002, p.1)

Bracken, whose book is a refreshingly positive account of the Descartes story, should have written "Attempted refutations continue to pile up." The truth is that Descartes was 100% correct on the two 'threads' of his revolutionary discoveries.

In fact, all three members of the British Empiricist Triumvirate, namely, Locke, Berkeley, and Hume, accepted his conclusion that we have no direct contact with realities outside our mind. Immanuel Kant, like his early hero, Leibniz, took seriously the challenge posed by Descartes, namely, "What then is reality like and how can we know it?", and with his *Critique of Pure Reason* changed forever the course of Western thought.

More remarkably still, Albert Einstein studied Kant in his youth, agreed with the conclusion of Descartes, and offered his own semi-Kantian solution to the challenge.

Finally, William James (1842-1910), the greatest thinker of all—greatest partly because, with the exception of Einstein and other twentieth-century thinkers, he had access to the further discoveries of Locke, etc.—based his monumental masterpiece, *The Principles of Psychology*, on Descartes' mind-brain model.

Descartes Vindicated. Between 1985 and 1995, I wrote three books, none of them ever published, to show how one could synthesize the valid convictions of our early common-sense worldview or philosophy with the great insights of William James' psychology. The first was by far the longest (600 pages with small print), and each of the next two became shorter and shorter. In the summer of 1995, I decided to write a very brief abridgement of the main ideas presented in those longer works. Several students, after taking a course of mine, have read *Re-Meditations*, and have wondered why I've never used it in any of my courses. I suppose it's been because it had to cover so much material in too brief a fashion.

But thanks to the advent of inexpensive, on-demand self-publishing, it is time to try and show why Descartes was (largely) correct in his revolutionary conclusions about the state of our knowledge vis-à-vis reality. It has never been more important to bring his message to the educated public. This will be the seventh book of mine to be published in the last five years, five of them self-published. Where the details for what follows are not known by any readers, a large supply of them can be found in those other books.

Why Descartes is more important than ever. The reason is simple. As Harry Bracken noted, more and more recent authorities have attacked Descartes. As a consequence, most readers will decide it is a waste of time to study Descartes' masterworks.

Richard Watson, an unregenerate naive realist, thought by some to have written the 'definitive' biography of Descartes, obviously did not take Descartes' arguments seriously. But he did understand perfectly the reason why Descartes is so important. He explains that reason at length in the conclusion to his book, *Cogito, Ergo Sum: a Life of René Descartes.* Here are the first and last paragraphs of his book:

> René Descartes's *Discourse on Method* was published in 1637 and his *Meditations on First Philosophy* in 1641. Both books have been in print ever since. Descartes's mathematical method and mind-body metaphysics have directed the course of Western philosophy and science now for three and a half centuries. I remarked in the introduction that our whole Western culture— both humanistic and technological—is Cartesian to the core. So it is not surprising that Descartes's ideas also set the agenda for the twenty-first century, for a great battle. The results of that battle will lead to the greatest revolution that humankind will ever undergo. That battle is the last battle for the human soul...
>
> In the twenty-first century, this is how the last battle for the human soul will go. Materialists will discover more and more about how the brain works. Mentalists will never be able to show how an

independent mind works. One day, one hundred, two hundred years down the line, everyone will finally realize that the materialists have won and that the mentalists have lost this last battle for the human soul. When humankind finally faces the fact that the mind is the brain, that there is no independently existing mental soul to survive the death of the body, that none of us chirpy sparrows is immortal, when Descartes's ghost in the machine finally fades away and his animal machine is triumphant, then there will be a revolution in human thought the like of which none has gone before. (R. Watson, *Cogito Ergo Sum*, pp.312 and 326.)

More of Watson's worldview philosophy is on display in the introduction to which his conclusion refers. Compare it with the worldview philosophy you will learn about in the following pages. For instance:

Socrates advocated the principle my country right or wrong and accepted a death sentence he thought unjust rather than support civil disobedience, yet few people see him as the intellectual giant behind Stalinist totalitarianism. Jesus started a religion one of whose most distinguishing characteristics is the presentation of women, marriage, and human sexuality as evil, and in whose name hundreds of millions of people have been slaughtered, yet Christianity is revered as a religion of love. If we are to blame the ills of the modern world on great dead white men, Socrates and Jesus have as much to answer for as does Descartes. But neither of them gets near the bad press as Descartes does. Our hero is a real bad man. (Watson, *Same*, p.21)

But what if Socrates and Jesus are to be thanked rather than reviled for their courageous refusal to be silenced by hostile critics? Then—sorry, Richard—Descartes is also to be thanked, not reviled. Our hero was not a bad man. As for you...

INTRODUCTION

Half of me wants to do for you what I have been doing for many who agreed back in July and August to read *Re-Meditations* before I revised them. That half wants to give you a simple picture to keep in front of you while you toil at the task of reading what follows. Here's the picture. Latest estimates of the world population hover around 5.7 billion earthlings. If we were all attending a world conference in the Sahara Desert, you would see that many human bodies of all ages, sizes, weights, skin-color, and so on. Descartes, in his 1641 *Meditations*, proposed that the bodies are not the persons. The persons are immaterial, spiritual beings 'inhabiting' the bodies. Whoever reads R.Moody's *Life After Life* reports of people who claim to have died for a time and then returned to their bodies can easily connect Descartes' theory and those reports. And believe that they are possible. In fact, millions upon millions of people believe in reincarnation which also connects directly with Descartes' theory. After all, the person—say, your great grandmother—who might now be living in a male body (maybe even a male cow's body?) is clearly an invisible being distinct from the previous female and present male body. What's more, the idea of reincarnation is familiar to everyone who studies Plato's writings and tries to decide whether he tended to believe in it as all of his words suggest or surreptitiously argued against it as some of our 'experts' suggest.

There's more to the simple picture, however. Besides picturing yourself as an immaterial, spiritual being living inside your body, you must add the idea of "consistent hallucination." The body you think you feel is really only a huge hallucination. If you read up on reports of amputees who experience 'phantom-limbs,' you will understand why Descartes said that our body-sensations are not proof that we have a body. People without arms can feel 'arms,' amputees with no legs can feel 'legs,' and O.Sacks, in *A Leg to Stand On*, told how he both had a leg he could not feel and felt a 'leg' he did not have. Once you have absorbed that astonishing lesson, you will be ready to understand why Albert Einstein asked Abraham Pais whether he really believed the moon exists only when he looked at it. Ever since Descartes put physics and physiology together, clear-thinking scientists have known why everyone from Descartes to Kant has wondered whether our perceptions of the physical world are only a consistent hallucination. And we who live at the end of this century can learn why the Star-Trek idea of holodecks—rooms equipped to produce all kinds of hallucinatory experiences on command—is solid-science fiction*. That is, by becoming familiar with the virtual-reality technology, you will understand the science behind the fiction. (*The real question is—as you will see— "Is it fiction? ")

Sum it up. The simple picture to keep beside you at all times while you are reading is this. You are really an angel experiencing a virtual-reality 'world.' And virtual-reality 'people.' In short, you are an angel experiencing a consistent hallucination. And you should be trying to figure out what's really going on outside your private virtual-reality. Your unique life-movie.

The other half of me wants to tell you that today's experts think Descartes' theory has been decisively disproven. The 4-20-92 *Newsweek* carried an essay attached to its cover-story on the brain. The title of the essay was "Is the Mind an Illusion? ", and what followed gave the answer "Yes, say the philosopher-scientists. The brain is a machine. We have no selves, no souls. " The essay went on to say that Gilbert Ryle delivered the *coup de grace* to Descartes' theory, adding that "Dualists [followers of Descartes] nowadays are considered as obsolete as manual typewriters. " Clearly, though, those academic philosopher-scientists who believe Ryle delivered a *coup de grace* have not yet discovered that contemporary 'demolitions' of Descartes' theory were themselves utterly demolished in 1967 by Jonathan Harrison when he published his brilliant science-fiction* rebuttal entitled "A Philosopher's Nightmare: or, The Ghost Not Laid. " This other half of me wants to tell you about his story and how tightly it fits with these *Re-Meditations,* but the first half of me used up more than its half of the room for this foreword. (*Same footnote as above.)

Both halves of me join together, however, in wanting to alert you to a great and present danger. More and more people are coming to believe that Descartes was wrong. And, if a day arrives when everyone believes that, our world will be in worse shape than when everyone believed that it was flat.

PREFACE

Hello. (Again?) Might as well get right to it. Where is that "Hello" from? Whose voice is it? When we dial our voice-mail telephone number at school, a pleasant voice says "Hello." It is clearly a woman's voice, just as clearly as it is a man's voice on every Perry Como CD, cassette, or record. (Which, tho, is a speechless person's computer-generated 'voice'?) This book has *one predominant aim*: to help you answer the question, "Where is that above 'Hello' coming from?" It is to help you pass the Turing Test designed to see whether you can identify the voice of a non-machine person, as opposed to that of a non-person machine such as a computer.

(Or) Has God ever spoken to you? Directly? The way God allegedly spoke to Moses, Mohammed, and Koresh? Naturally, atheistic believers believe God didn't speak to anyone. How can someone who doesn't exist do any speaking? Theistic believers don't believe every claim that God has spoken to someone is true. The catechism teachers taught me that God did not speak to Mohammed, and most people feel quite confident God didn't speak to David. But theist believers believe that God can speak to anyone at all, if that's what God decides to do. So, has God ever spoken to you? If you are wondering why atheists are called believers, it is for the same reason I grew up believing women were men. That is, we were taught that "All men are mortal" applied to all humans in general, the way evolutionists think humans are animals when they say "All animals are the product of evolution." An atheist who believes there are no divine persons but cannot prove it is a believer.

(Or, in case that didn't get your attention...) Human reason has this peculiar fate that in one species of its knowledge it is burdened by questions which, as prescribed by the very nature of reason itself, it is not able to ignore, but which, as transcending all its powers, it is also not able to answer. (Did you recognize Kant's voice here? This is a copy of paragraph one from his major *Critique* as translated by Smith.)

A thesis. The scientific truth of the matter is that not only does God speak to everyone, but God alone does it. Directly. Individually. This book will offer a proof for that truth. That is, it will put into your possession an argument or line of reasoning that can, once you are thoroughly familiar with all its parts, convince you that *God is the source of every thought* that anyone ever understands. Just the way God—not some human person—is the source of the thoughts coming to you right now. Every educated person knows that science is full of surprises. In physics, you learned that what you think is a solid book with solid pages is more full-of-holes than a piece of swiss cheese. Once you learn all about modern physiology in its essentials, you'll know why you can be more sure of God than of books, of God than of the eyes and hands you think you see and touch books with. People think God speaks mostly through a voice from a burning bush or a cloud, or through visions or dreams, but that's because they have pre-scientific notions about bushes and clouds, visions and dreams. It is time to be scientific all the way and to recognize that all scientific truths are direct revelations from God. All errors come directly from God, too.

These remeditations will argue *for* that view and *against* its 'incommensurable' competitors, and this preface just offered you the conclusion of the argument. Here is another of its conclusions: *every argument is circular*, therefore this preface is part of a circle of conclusion-premises. Many prefaces are written only after the rest of the book is already finished. It is easy to understand why. A description of what you intend to write is easier to write after you've done the writing. No book I have ever written has turned out the way I planned it. And this preface will not be exactly as I planned it, since I have planned it only in a very general way. I do, however, already know the things I believe, and I have just told you two of them.

Here I another conclusion I will prove. It's one that took me many years to finally realize, which is why it is fitting to call it a conclusion. Prefaces and books do not exist. If you have already scanned the rows and rows of 'print' that follow, you will appreciate why the non-existence of prefaces and books follows logically from or is contained in another major premise to be explained as you read along, namely, that *language as such does not exist*. And you will also know why that conclusion-premise is so important that, in the non-pages that follow, language will be or has been called "the Last of the Great Myths." That part of this extended argument is so important that it deserves a special, dramatic cue like that. Were Francis Bacon writing this, he would call language "the Last of the Great Idols of the Mind." The last, and in a sense, the most confusion-creating, since the Myth of Language is the prop for all the other Idols of the Mind.

That part of this extended argument probably needs a few more preliminary words. Till we liberate ourselves from the vise-grip of myths about language and names, we tend to proceed as if every name must be the name for something, else how could it be a name? Which would mean then that language does exist and is not a fiction. How can language be a fiction, that is, not exist, since we have a name for it? Consider, though, that we have a name for nothing, too, but it cannot exist, since—if it did—it would be something. Of course, if you have finished reading what I have not yet begun to write (this preface is a prescript, not a postscript, and was begun earlier today, Saturday, May twenty-seventh, nineteen-ninety-five), then you will know more of the circular argument cued and clued by what follows to explain why language and the words which allegedly—but don't—'make it up' do not exist. And more about why names, which are part of language, don't, either. Not the name for names. Nor the name for what-doesn't-exist in general, namely, "nothing."

The discovery that what "language" names is a fiction, that is, that "language" cues a thought about something that does not exist, gives those of us living at this end of the twentieth and greatest of centuries an enormous advantage over our ancestors, of whom William James was one. Unlike them and him, we have in our libraries an enormous collection of non-writings about language left there by writers referred to by such non-names as "logical positivists," "the ordinary language school," "the analytic school," and so on. A more generic non-name cue for a mental grouping of their efforts to turn the tide of western thought away from thought and to language is "the Linguistic Turn." A thorough immersion in the conclusion-premises of those who took part in that failed turn or revolution is probably the best vaccination against the Idols of the Mind imaginable, since it helps us learn how endless are the fictions which the human mind or imagination is able to get trapped by, including those cued by "mind," "imagination," especially "letters," "words," "sentences," "paragraphs," and a mountain of other 'language'-related fictions. Unmasking such fictions or analysing such thoughts about things which do not exist is a critical part of the process of discovering the truth about what does exist. Unfortunately, those who took part in the twentieth-century's abortive linguistic revolution failed to realize that language itself—or "language" itself—cues a 'theoretical fiction' that calls for ruthless analysis. If anything cries out to be recognized for what it is, if any spade demands to be called "a spade," so that we can turn our thoughts from non-words to thoughts which are distinct from them, it is *what you see* whenever you go to the library and do what you're doing right now. Till we brush away the cobwebs of fantasy about 'insights that can't be put into words' (there are no words to put any insights into), fictions about 'insights' (as if reason's not their source), poetry about 'the heart' (as if it's distinct from that other fiction, 'the head'), and others, we will never be able to sit down with one another and decide who sees things as they are and whose 'bedrock convictions' are half-truths or less.

You and I do live at this end of the twentieth century, th<u>ow</u>. That makes it possible for us to demythologize langwidge and thereby to become more super-resistant to the th<u>aw</u>t-traps begot by langwidge-traps than Descartes, James, and others of our ancestors were. That, in turn, makes it possible for us to more confidently answer the major kwestions which every scientist must answer. You will or do know that, to the kwestion "How many major kwestions are there?", this circular argument offers the answer "Only three." They are: What exists?, What does what-exists do?, and Why? These remeditations have, as one of their chief aims, to argue that, to the "What exists?" kwestion, "Zillions of things, which can nevertheless be mentally grouped into five classes" is the most useful answer. Which five? "Sense-data" is the non-name for the easiest-to-notice, "thawts" the name for the most-difficult-to-notice but more significant, of the categories. "Persons" names the most basic class. "Omidges"—women's and men's—cues the fourth species of existing existents. (The o's are pronounced the same.) And, if bodies exist, "subatoms" is the best english (non)symbol for the fifth type. The five items make up a list that is almost as easy to remember as the ancients' table of elements. Thairz wuz air, earth, fire, and water. Ourz is persons, thawts, what we sense, omidges, and sub-atom-sized bodies. Since kwestions are not on the list, of course, kwestions as such do not exist, even thow "kwestion" can be used as a (non)name for other things (other than langwidge) as such, much the same way as rittun and spowken langwidges as such do not exist, even thow *seen* ciphers and *heard* sounds as sensed-things do. Only by acquiring the second-nature habit of recognizing such facts as redally as we recognize that a 'hotel' on a monopoly board is no hotel **as such** but only a piece of red plastic **as such**, will reeders ever get down to the reel business of correctly counting and classifying everything that exists and unbelieving in fictitious entities. That is...

Only by becoming fluent in 'reading' rows and rows of 'print' such as the ones that preceded will you recognize instantly that "ow" and "aw" substituted for "ough" and "ough," two completely *similar* parts of visible, *written* language (the english species) supposed to go with completely *different* parts of audible, *spoken* english. And only by knowing some history of our crazily-conjugated and just-as-crazily-written* english will you understand why we use "thought" as the past tense of "think" and why we use "though" for one sound but "though+t" for that very different one. Becoming fluent in such thoughts will take a lot of stop-to-think'ing. My aim will be to provide you with assistance, your aim must be to do it often enough to acquire the necessary thought-habits. Speaking of aims, the one spoken of in the first paragraph is mine, not the remeditations', a point crucial to another thesis of this book. One that goes to the very core of this preface and...

God. (At least to the core of *your ideas about* the author of this preface and God.) Aims, motives, or intentions belong exclusively to persons. Only persons have the knowledge required to consciously and deliberately intend some end or goal, that is, the pre-knowledge required to aim in the present at a goal to be reached only in the future. This preface is partly motivated by my present desire to draw your (future) attention to its relation to the remeditations which follow. STOP. Think about that claim. Or, what means the same thing (here, where I know perfectly what I am thinking and mean to have you think), take a moment and meditate on the relation of what I am here and now declaring before I compose the six chapters which follow to those six chapters which you will be holding in your hand even as you read this preface which refers to them. By helping you more fully grasp the complex concept of motivation which is at the core of humans' lives, it will help you learn better about God. Who had a pre-plan and had decided what to do before ever creating us humans. Let me be even more direct. By calling a spade "a spade." (*Language is referred to as conventional signs, viz., as signs agreed to by 'society.' It is distinguished from natural signs, the way smoke is a sign of fire. But in every case, as we'll see, it's mere habits of association.)

Buddhists are atheists, and buddhism is a religion without a deity. Those are two claims made by many experts. Both claims, if unqualified, can foster harmful mis-conceptions. There are Buddhists and then there are Buddhists, and some are better thought of as crypto-Jews, -Christians, -Moslems, or -theists. Vice-versa is also true. (A rose by any other name looks and smells just the same.) The question is not what a person is called or what language is used to do the calling. The question is what can you tentatively expect the next Buddhist to believe that is different from what you expect most Jews, Christians, Moslems, or just plain theists to believe. The Jewish scriptures talk about God as a person: all-powerful, all-knowing, all-loving, and so on. Christians get their name from the greatest of the Jewish teachers, one who consistently spoke of God as a male parent with whom we can be so intimate that we can address him as "Papa," the way people who revere parents they feel are immeasurably superior can still address them as "Mom" and "Dad." Most Moslems' idea of God is like that of most Jews and most Christians. Etc. Whether the being believed in is referred to by this or that name—Yahweh, Adonai, Our Father, Allah, etc.—is crucial only to those who believe names exist. The thought's the thing, not the name.

Person. That's the english name that's most important for God. God is a person. In fact, one reason Jews and Moslems object to Christians' belief-system is that most Christians believe there are three divine persons. Apart from those who regard this as blasphemy, everyone who first learns about the Christians' faith is very, very mystified: how can there be one divine being but three divine persons? Christians defend their belief the way all of us do when we discover that two of our basic beliefs appear to be in direct conflict with each other: they call it a mystery. Or conundrum. Or paradox. Every belief-system is chock full of them. Be clear, then. Those called "Buddhist" who believe there is a divine being who can speak and be understood the way you think you can is a theist who believes God is as much a person as you or I, and those who call themselves "Jew," "Christian," "Moslem," etc., and think the way a-theist Buddhists think are a-theists. That's what I believe. And, this preface is meant to tell you beforehand what I intend to tell you after this preface is done, so you will be able to meditate on what it means to think before-hand about what you commit yourself in the present to doing at some point in the future. His ability to do that will be evidence that **Hello**'s author is a person. One of the greatest merits of James' writings is the fact that he wrote more about goal-pursuing than Descartes did, even though the idea is central to Descartes' *Meditations.*

Let me elaborate. Descartes, who argued that God is too good to be a deceiver, lived when people accepted the *Genesis* story of a world completed in six days or—for fear of reprisals—did not dare to attack it openly. James, on the other hand, grew up in a century when the steady-state view of the universe was being replaced by a dynamic one. Kant had spoken of celestial bodies evolving from spiralling clouds of matter, Hegel had popularized the idea that the universe is a living, organic whole growing toward maturity, and Darwin—when James was seventeen—had seemingly proved that every species evolved from an undifferentiated beginning. The new picture of a universe which was not created in six days by an omni-competent, outside person, but which evolved from an initially formless state *like a self-hatching egg* by virtue of blind, internal forces, so weakened traditional beliefs that Nietzsche declared "God is dead, and we have killed him." It was only natural that James would wonder, as do so many today, whether there is any cosmos-sized Mind capable of having a plan for this universe and any cosmos-sized Power capable of guiding it to the pre-planned goal. If the non-name "God" refers (via your thought) to a being even remotely similar to the one most of our western ancestors believed in, that being has a plan and has motives for creating. Plans and motives are inextricably linked to pre-thought. And only persons are capable of pre-thoughts. That thought is pure commonsense. It is time to be more thoroughly scientific and stop using the familiar name "God" for what Einstein and so many other a-theist believers use it for. Or, at least, to have better—that is, truer—beliefs than they. On the whole, that is.

It has long been the custom in some quarters to think that God has authored two great books. The first is the book called *The Bible*. It has been and continues to be regarded by millions as one of the means whereby God intends to reveal the Divine Self to us. The second is nature, which has been and continues to be regarded by millions as a means, in part, whereby God intends to reveal the Divine Self to us. We are ready now for the final scientific revelation that neither bible nor nature as such exist, since only persons (divine and human), thoughts, images, sense-data, and (possibly) subatom-sized bodies exist as such. Such a revelation can radically change your way of interpreting what you are doing and experiencing right now. And now. And now. Etc.

Whether you agree or not, do you at least understand?

Conclusion. Of this preface. Or stepping stone to Re-Meditation I. On May 27, 1995, I am predicting that, beginning on Monday (I rest on the Sabbath), I will write six chapters to make a Grand-Unified-Theory-of-Everything-type 'case' to show that the Divine Self is behind every "hello." As well as behind every other seen cipher and heard sound that we mis-take for words. If I am not a machine but a free agent able to pursue future aims and choose the means which seem best suited to achieve them, that means that what follows can be seen—understood—as carrying out in deed or practice or praxis what does not yet exist except in thought or contemplation. I will complete *Re-Meditations'* lines in a way that makes them dovetail with what you see at the head of this preface so that you will understand why I added or what was my motive for adding "(Again?)."

Note. Suppose I had not corrected "4-20-93" in the Foreword and suppose you had gone to the library to read the *Newsweek* essay it referred to. You would have discovered that there was no 4-20-93 issue with a cover story on the brain. If you were an experienced library-user, you would have checked the bound volumes for the years 1990, 1991, 1992, 1994, and 1995, and discovered that the issue referred to was published in 1992, not 1993. You would have lost some time, but not nearly as much as an inexperienced person would have lost. There would have been some harm done, but not much. Imagine the harm done to unwise library users who gullibly believe what misguided teachers send them—with perfectly accurate instructions as to sources and dates—to read and learn. End of note.

I. YOUR SINGLE COSMIC-SPACE FRAMEWORK

One. Space as the setting for history. (Instruction: just try to understand, not argue.) What exists? That is the first and most basic question of all. As will be shown, the thought that there is one, single container for everything that exists is a very useful idea. Whatever you think exists, you can—if you freely choose to do so—think of in relation to some exact location in space or to some thing so located. If you think of something that does not seem to be anywhere, think of it in relation to your self.

Where are you? Picture yourself located in the middle of *your* 'world.' Other folks are somewhere else. Even during your most unselfish and self-forgetful moments, the ground you'll feel will be the particular ground that is under your feet, not those of the other person(s) you are paying attention to. Get in the habit of noticing that. If your head gets lost in the clouds, the clouds in question will be the ones in contact with you, and the only part of the clouds your head will touch will be the parts right next to your head. If you get lost in thoughts and wonder where the thoughts are located, get in the habit of thinking that they are somewhere on your in- and not your out-side. Your skin is in between those two sides, you can relate your in- and out-sides to the two sides of your skin, and you can put both thoughts together by thinking that your skin is protecting your insides from the outside surroundings.

From you at its center, space spreads outward in every direction. Infinitely. Which means space is boundaryless or endless. To gear yourself up for modern science, you must get in the habit of imagining you have imaginary lines running through you. One comes right into your chest and goes out in back, another comes from the right and continues on to your left, and the third comes from above your head and keeps going downward through your feet. Pretend all three lines meet at a single point somewhere inside you. The marvel of mathematical physics is that, by referring to those three lines, you can describe the exact location of every body in relation to you(rs). Again, things that lack their own location are related to bodies that have a location. These thoughts of yours are an example.

Two. History of space. (This is a set-up.) How old is space? If you decide to go to the library and look up the answer to that question, you will find that authors do not agree. That is what makes such questions interesting. There are so many different ways of looking at everything. As a jury of one, you must decide which way's right.

Those who believe that God created everything and that everything God created is just so old and no older, believe that space is only as old as the other things God created. Those who think that "space" means "the sum total of all the distance-plus-direction relations between three-dimensional bodies" have to believe that, because there couldn't be any relations before there were related things. Other people think that space is a separate thing. If space were only a whole lot of relations, then it would follow that space depends on the related things. No one can be an uncle before he has a niece or nephew, and no single body, say a billiard ball, can be six inches or six feet off to the left of something if the billiard ball is the only body in existence. But you can imagine the Creator creating only one billiard ball, can't you? Unless space is a separate reality, then that billiard ball would not exist in space and it would be unable to move an exact distance and direction in it. People who think like this can say that God created space along with bodies so that there would be a receptacle for them, or—like Plato (cfr. *Timaeus*)—they can think space always existed, since—if space had to be created so God would have somewhere to put bodies, then—God would need an older space to put the new space into. Newton skirted all such problems by simply asserting the existence of one 'absolute space' and making it the setting for his whole physics. Still, any way you think of it, puzzles will arise.

Think of how puzzling the idea of space is. We use it in contradictory ways. Do you have any closets that are nearly full? That barely have any space left in them? If, during your spring cleaning, you take a lot of junk out of the closet, do you have any more space than you had before? Or do you have just as much space, but more of it is empty? (Does putting another object into the closet squeeze some of the space out, the way water in a full tub spills over the side if someone steps into it?) Is the empty space different from the full space, or is all space just plain space, no matter whether something is in it or not? Add library-contained discussions of place to the debates about space, the way I was taught to, and things get complex, indeed.

Three. Start to revise your Big Picture. I'm not sure I ever heard a single discussion of space until I was over twenty. I know I took a course in physics before that, but I have no recollection whatever of any discussion of space as such. When I did begin studying it, was I ever naive! I was ready to believe in tons of things that never did and never will exist, e.g., such things as space, history, physics, courses, and so on. Even concepts. For instance, Section Two was not about what its title predicted. It was about contradictory concepts of space, not about its history. There is a difference between real things and our concepts about them. Take the stars, for instance. The stars existed long before any humans did, before there were concepts (imagined parts of thoughts) about stars. Is astronomy about astronomy or about stars? You will avoid a lot of problems if you memorize one simple rule: a *real thing* and a *real concept* of that real thing add up to two real things, not one. Non-concept realities and real concepts are (for now) distinct species of the generic class of realities-period!

Here is a second confusion-avoiding rule: keep three, not just one or two, items sorted out in your thinking: **reality** (what exists—period!), **thoughts** (your concepts, presumably about reality), and **language** (symbols for your concepts). For instance, look at the last paragraph in section two and its beginning: "Think of how puzzling the idea of space is. We use it in contradictory ways."

How clear are your answers to the following questions? QU: Do we use space in contradictory ways? Or the idea of space? Or the word "space"? ONE AN: When you go to look up others' answers, you will find that there's no consensus. In this century, there are large numbers of authors who thought, as I <u>do</u>, that concepts do not literally exist, large numbers who think, as I do <u>not</u>, that when we talk about words' meanings, we are actually talking about words and how we use them, but not many who think, as I do, that words do not exist. As for space: there's no reality, concept, or word, but it is extremely useful and even indispensable to get in the habit of often pretending that all three are real.

Thesis. Everything that exists is already known by somebody. Most puzzles—not all!, though—are caused, not by lack of knowledge of what exists, but *by too many beliefs* in mythical things that do not.

The task, then, is to unmask fictions. Parmenides claimed that what-is-not can't be, can't be thought, and can't be named. Maybe not. But we understand thoughts 'about' what does not exist. When mom tells us <u>that</u> Santa exists, we understand her. If names and ideas existed, we'd say that the name "Santa" exists, that ideas of Santa exist, even though Santa does not exist. At least not Santa as such. The real universe may contain lots of pictures of Santa, lots of men dressed up like Santa, lots of people with lots of thoughts about Santa, lots of books with stories and poems about Santa, and so on. Just no Santa. (To understand the beliefs of atheists, just replace "Santa" with "God.") Whatever does not exist—space!—has no history.

Four. Classify correctly the things in your model.
The theory presented in these *Re-Meditations* is that, at most, only five types of things exist: persons, thoughts, sense-data, quasi-copy-images of previously-sensed data, and (possibly) sub-atom-sized bodies. One logical implication of that claim is that, if the list is complete and space is not on it, then space does not exist. Understanding or making sense of this claim calls for an effort to be as utterly clear as possible about real things that do exist vs fictions which do not. If we can be grateful to Freud for making us super-conscious of our unnoticed (not unconscious!) motivations and excuse him for all of his nonsense, then we can also thank Parmenides for bringing it to our attention that there are no such things as things that do not exist, that is, no such thing as what-is-not, and forgive him for wrapping that insight in absurd monistic fluff. To get clear on the difference between (thoughts about) what exists and (thoughts about) what doesn't, it helps to call on imagination...

Picture yourself as someone who is a learner attempting to create an accurate inner model or representation of everything in the universe. A single inner model. A single total representation. Imagine that deciding what exists is deciding what to put into your inner model or representation. Deciding something is a fiction means, in part, deciding to remove it. The most important challenges are two: try not to keep something out just because you are in the habit of thinking it cannot exist, and try not to remove things that do exist when you remove things that do not. For many people, the decision to eliminate God is so habitual that it would be a miracle if they reconsidered.

For others, removing language and words will seem to be removing what they see (it seems these are words, right?) and what they hear. To understand the 'case' for this five-types view will require a dramatic revision of the everyday view you will unhesitatingly revert to when you put this book down, and both those challenges will have to be faced when you pick it up again. The revision can be—in fact, it must be—approached gradually. It will require taking items from your present, commonsense view of things and putting them into the new model, and then, as the revision continues, removing some of the things transported from the old into the new model, until the revision is done and you can compare the two models side-by-side to decide which is the true one.

One more preliminary is this. You will have to learn about classifying. There are simply too many things in the universe to deal with each one individually. Dealing with that difficulty is not only easy. It is something everyone learns to do at a very early age. We learn to classify things which are alike by making a class or group of them. Mentally. (E.g., ladies and gentlemen.) We can mentally group those groups. (E.g., the human race.) We can even mentally group things and declare that they are not a group while doing so. (E.g., the chaos of truths and errors.)

The grouping that is *most basic of all* is the one we do when we say something exists or decide something does not exist. Here is a way to picture the claim that only five classes of things exist. Imagine you have a real blackboard in front of you. Draw a line down its middle. Imagine that, at the top of the left half, you write "What exists" and, at the top of the right half, "What does not exist." Under

"What exists," group the five (types of) items listed above: persons, thoughts, sense-data, memory-images, and subatoms. Under "What does not exist," write the labels for everything else. Including "lists," "labels," "diagrams," and so on. Be careful, however, not to write on the right names which are merely synonyms for persons, thoughts, and so on. For instance, "remeditations" goes on the left, not the right. *But only if!* That is, only if "remeditations" is used as a synonym for "thoughts" or "theories." But if you find "remeditations" used in a context which indicates that it is a synonym for "the words in this book," then it goes on the right half with such non-names as "words," "book," "synonyms," "halves," "names," and....

And "space." The non-word "space" goes on the right with the other non-names for things that do not exist. That creates a problem, though. What should you do with fictions, that is, with things that do not exist? The answer is simple. A fiction can be sneaked onto the left side of your mental diagram by going to the word "thoughts" and finding a place to insert it there. (Thoughts about things that do not exist have been coming to you while you've been reading, haven't they?) Fitting fictions or figments of our imagination into our one model of the universe is easy. If we can group things mentally, we can also ungroup them. In this case, we ungroup all the *different* thoughts we have mentally lumped into the *same or one* group, thoughts-in-general. *Sub-divide the genus-group of thoughts into species-groups:* a-thoughts about things that once existed but no longer do, b-thoughts about things that do not yet exist but will, c-thoughts about things that never did, do not, and never will, and d-thoughts about the only things that really exist, viz., those which exist right now. Now *every*thing that does not exist can be put under what does. *"Space" fits quite nicely among your* **thoughts** *about things that never did, do not, and never will exist,* because you can think very complicated, extremely useful, even indispensable thoughts about the imaginary space which exists in between the bodies it contains.

First, though, a few pieces of advice. Do not worry for now about "If space does not exist, how did I get my idea of it?" Or, if you can't help it, just keep repeating (for now) that you created it with your powerful imagination. Second, do not ask "Would any expert agree with this?" Or, if the question does nag at you, assume that the true answer is "Some would and some would not." There is not a single part of this overall theory that has not been put forth at least tentatively by some expert and that has not been absolutely blasted by some other, even—in many cases—by an expert repudiating later a belief s/he put forth earlier. Join those two pieces of advice into a third one: concentrate all your efforts for now on trying to follow the exposition that follows. Once you feel confident you have understood a new idea, meditate on it, try to understand how it fits with earlier ideas, and pray that such trying will help you remember it when it becomes a crucial premise for correctly understanding a later conclusion. A fourth, perhaps the most important, suggestion is to think of this as a roller-coaster ride. Let yourself go as you career ahead. Let your mind, temporarily at least, race right past the objections that are sure to leap out from every side. Unless you suffer total amnesia, you'll remember them well enough to return later and give them the attention they deserve. Back then to (thoughts about) space. Which doesn't exist. Though thoughts about it do.

Five. Pretend that space is a universal container. It is easy. Space is a useful concept. Newton based his physics on it and Kant saw spread-out-ness as basic to experience. To get used to the idea, think how easy it is to understand thoughts about things that do not exist. Shakespeare wrote a play, *Romeo and Juliet*, about people who, so far as I know, never lived. If I enrolled in a course on Shakespeare, I'd realize once and for all whether the teacher and I agree, just as soon as s/he said "*Romeo and Juliet* is fiction." The teacher would not have to constantly refer to "the fictitious Romeo" and "the fictitious Juliet" or to "the nonexistent Montagues" and "the imaginary Capulets." Think: adults can tell lies galore to children about Santa Claus without once suffering an attack of doubt about Santa's nonexistence. As you read what follows about space, just pretend that you are reading about something purely imaginary. As imaginary as inky black, utterly dark, completely empty nothingness.

Do not begin thinking of space, though, until you know where you would find it, if it existed. Begin rather by calling up on the screen of your imagination a picture of all the things that seem most certainly to exist. There is no better way to do this than the way new disciples of Aristotle, groomed to become "neo-Aristotelians," are taught to begin: with the spread-out, apparently-three-dimensional things you see, touch, etc. With the things you can be sure are real because you sense them.

Which of the things you sense should you begin with? In order to make space your one huge container of everything, start with the stars in the sky which you look at from the earth. The stars in the night sky are so awesome that Immanuel Kant referred to them as one of the two most awesome things he could think of. (Learn to appreciate what Kant meant. The night sky is a classic illustration for the saying that familiarity breeds contempt [in the thoughtless]. Emerson reflected on what would happen if the stars were to appear only one night every thousand years, and whoever can recall what happens each seventy-sixth year when Halley's Comet reappears can easily believe that every street would be crowded with people eager to get a glimpse of the stars.) Now, using the picture of the star-studded night sky which the words of this paragraph just called up on the screen of your imagination, you can locate invisible space. Just pretend that, wherever you see no stars and no anything-else, there is an invisible, intangible, undetectable stuff called "space."

Starting that way amounts to making astronomy the science which provides the framework for all the others. **Decide what you believe in.** How about the things that are farthest away, the stars in the night sky? How about the closest, the earth beneath your feet? Finally, and most important, how about you, on the earth, not up in the sky? If you adopt all three, *make a picture that situates each of those three in relation to the others.* Now add space as a fluid kind of stuff that spreads out everywhere, seeping into whatever nooks and crannies it can find. Very little imagination is needed to picture space as an ocean that is larger than any other single thing imaginable. If it fills the empty areas between earth and stars, it is large enough to hold every thing that any scientist has any visible evidence for. In fact, it takes very little extra imagination to think of it as continuing around to the back of the stars and extending outward, farther and farther, as far as imagination can go. Why, in other words, can't you imagine space as infinitely large? Large enough to contain everything that you believe could ever possibly exist?

Six. Become exact the way physicists are. "Large" is vague. "Infinitely large" is not really any better. Modern astronomy makes things more concrete. Start with what seems like a plain, everyday fact: no one has ever gotten close enough to a star to touch it. That fact led our most distant ancestors to realize stars are very far away. But, like many theists who don't begin to grasp God, those distant ancestors didn't even begin to realize the true dimensions of cosmic space. You can, though, if you go to the library and read enough about modern astronomical physics.

The sun, it turns out, is nothing but a star. The nearest one. But still, so far away—93,000,000 miles away—that walking there would take a terribly long time. At 5mph, it would take 25 days to walk 3,000 miles, nonstop, from New York to Los Angeles. It would take more than 2,000 years or more than 20 100-year lifetimes to walk 93 million miles. Celestial distances computed in miles result in such large numbers that astronomers find it convenient, when speaking about stars farther away than the sun, to count in terms of travel-time. In terms of years, in fact. That is, in terms of the number of years it takes *invisible* light to travel from one place to another. Light travels much faster than humans walk. A human could make a trip, not just once from NYC to LA, but around the earth's equator seven times in one, single second if s/he could move as fast as an *invisible* ray of light. That means—given 60 x 60 x 24 x 365 seconds in a year—that a ray of *invisible* light can travel roughly six trillion miles in one year. That in turn means that, although a ray of *invisible* light takes only 8 minutes, not 20 100-year lifetimes, to travel the 93,000,000 miles from the nearest star to us, it takes 4.3 years or over a quarter of a million times as long to get to us from the second closest star, which is more than 25 trillion miles away. To get an idea of what an 'astronomically large' amount of invisible space there is, consider how far away the most distant stars are. Not 4.3 light-years away, but two to four+ billion times that far. Imagine a sphere with a radius of 10 to 20 billion x 365 x 24 x 60 x 60 x 186,000 miles, imagine filling it with invisible space, and you have an idea of how many cubic miles of imaginary space there may be, just inside the small, occupied-by-sense-verifiable-bodies area, which in turn is surrounded by the even more immense area of infinite, inky black, utterly dark space. Which doesn't exist. Though the thoughts that just came to you did and the present one does.

Incidentally, you do not have to take <u>all</u> of this on faith. You can check for yourself to see whether light is invisible. Assume there is light between this page and your eyes. See it? Look around. You'll see, *not light*, but *things*! Things you cannot see (which are therefore invisible) whenever there is no invisible light to make them visible. Next, look up at the bright moon on a clear night. Apart from the earth's long, tunnel-shaped shadow, the night sky is absolutely filled with invisible light coming from the sun which is behind, on the lit side of the earth. Some light lights the moon, which is why we can see it whenever it is not caught in the earth's long shadow, that is, when there is no eclipse. Light's invisibility is the reason ancient thinkers called the medium of sight "the transparent." Light is that, alright.

Seven. Appearances (errors) vs reality (truth). Astronomy not only provides an all-embracing context for all the sciences ("science" will often serve as shorthand for "the real truth about things"), but it is also confronts us in a massive way with the challenge posed both by Descartes' *Meditations* and these updates: will you trust the reasoning that uses clues furnished by the senses to overcome mistaken thought-habits in order to discover what is the truth? The only reason why the searchings labelled 'mathematical sciences' have been so successful is that they are the result of thinking as exactly as possible about what is actually observed in order to guess as exactly as possible about what is not observed. There is a difference. You may see the moon, maybe even the clouds and haze blocking it, but you will never see any of the light supposedly travelling between the sun and moon or the moon and earth. But, from what you do see, you can make guesses about the light.

Ponder some facts. The earth we live on **appears** gigantic. Far more gigantic than any star. Far more gigantic even than the sun as it sinks behind the earth's far-away horizon, more gigantic than the also-small moon as it rises from behind the same far-off horizon. Spend some time thinking hard about the sizes those things **appear** to have. Imagine what you would believe about the world in general, if you were living thousands of years ago: that there is an earth so vast that no one you know has ever seen all of it, a bright, ball-shaped sun that lights up the world each time it re-appears in the sky, a moon that is about the same size as the sun but not nearly so bright, and hundreds of tiny little stars that don't really light up the earth at all. I can imagine growing up in a tribe living in the deep jungle and never having it occur to me to wonder just what was under my feet. Can't you? Who of us can be sure that, even if no one else did, we at least would wonder what would be found if we kept digging downward? The brainstorm some ancient ancestor got, of us living on a thick saucer floating in space, required a huge leap of imagination. Of course, that leap raised a problem: just what holds this 'saucer' up? We library-users are so used to thinking the earth **really is** a sphere twirling every 24 hours as it makes its 365-day trip around the sun, that we smile when we read *Genesis* and notice that our ancestors naively thought the earth was like a flat saucer suspended motionless in space. But that is only because we are too unreflective to appreciate that invisible leap of imagination which no chimp could ever match. Lacking that reflectiveness, it is natural that we also lack the reflectiveness needed to realize what an even more huge, invisible leap of imagination is needed to wonder how a chimp's invisible imagination measures up to ours, a leap no chimp—unthinkingly glancing at the ground and at the sun and incapable of invisibly wondering which is larger and utterly unable to stand in invisible awe before creatures (e.g., our ancestors) able to do such invisible wondering—could ever make. Our habitual INattention to the gigantic contrast between how the earth, moon, sun, and stars always **appear** and how we book-readers invisibly think they **really are** is almost more scandalous than our ancestors' invisible musings about a saucer-shaped earth were naive.

Eight. Libraries as universal containers... If your memory is good, you will recall the preface's claim that words do not exist, which means that texts made up of words do not exist, which means that libraries have no texts in them. But, if there are no books in the library (do literature teachers use "text" and "book" synonymously?), can there be genuine libraries? If not, then QU: Why all the references to libraries and books? AN: For more than one reason or motive.

First, because our concepts of libraries and books and words are good examples of fictions needed to discover realities. Think of this as **a basic principle**: we would not learn anything more than beasts, if we lacked 'word-cues' for sense-related features of our thoughts. At first, the 'word-sounds' we hear do nothing but get 'associated' with items that we (really or apparently) experience for ourselves. If we grow up in the USA, we will learn to attach "star" to one of things we see, "sun" to another, and so on. Eventually, people can use such sounds to prompt or stimulate us to recall what we have seen. Later, they can use those prompts to help us form a picture or scene and, with it as a platform, prompt us to form new ideas of things that we, and most often they, have not experienced: "What's on the other side of the moon?", "Is that where ghosts live?", "Ever wonder what ghosts think about when they aren't appearing to people?" This can happen only after we have constructed an inner model of the outer world and 'pegged' certain 'word' prompts to its different parts. By learning to 'read,' we can use visual prompts for memories of sound-prompts for memories of everything we've ever experienced in order to learn all about new things similar to what we already know.

A more important reason for fixing on libraries and books is to propose a counter-challenge to the famous one Hume meant to leave in a book he seemed to write for the world's libraries. It became an inspiration for this century's Linguistic Turners:

> When we run over libraries, persuaded of these principles, what havoc must we make? If we take in our hand any volume; of divinity or school metaphysics, for instance; let us ask, *Does it contain any abstract reasoning concerning quantity or number?* No. *Does it contain any experimental reasoning concerning matter of fact and existence?* No. Commit it then to the flames: for it can contain nothing but sophistry and illusion.

With enough time in the library, you can learn that Hume was challenging readers to reject the appearance that books about God, immortality, souls—topics most people regard as matters of blind faith or abstract reason— literally make no sense, i.e., to recognize them as much ado about nothing, as sophistry (vain word games), or as illusion (deceptions). And then... You can learn what one contemporary theoretical physicist wrote in 1988 about physical bodies:

> Our mental pictures are drawn from our visual perceptions of the world around us. But the world as perceived by the eye is itself exposed as an illusion when scrutinized on the microscopic scale. A bar of gold, though it looks solid, is composed almost entirely of empty space. . . ; on the subatomic scale,

> [...] billiard balls are as spacious as galaxies, and were it not for their like electrical charges they could, like galaxies, pass right through each other unscathed. (T.Ferris, *Coming of Age in the Milky Way*, ch.15.)

Whoever takes Ferris' non-words seriously can understand why Hume's challenge is countered by a challenge to show that what appear to be libraries, books, hands, and flames are not—like bars of gold and billiard balls—really illusions. If physical bodies exist at all on the (be)yon(d) side of what you see, they are colorless, sub-microscopic in size, and rarely, if ever, collide with each other.

"It's a bird, it's a plane, it's Superman!" Slightly adapted—"It's a bird, it's a flock of birds, no, it's a squadron of planes..."—that line from the old Superman show will prime your imagination for the truth that **none of the objects you see is really one body and every body you think you can see is really zillions of never-seen bodies.** First, let it remind you how often what you think is a single thing turns out to be many. Then turn your thoughts to the things we call "stars." We are used to the idea that our sun is clearly a single star, separate from the billions that 'make up' the galaxy named "the Milky Way." If we could get as far away as the farthest star and look back, though, we would be unable to make out our sun, because the entire Milky-Way-ful of stars would look like one thing. But our sun-star and billions of others do not 'make up' one thing. They are just billions of individual stars, each of which is light years away from the others. But that is just the beginning.

There are no stars or planets, either. We here on the earth have learned the lesson referred to by Ferris by studying what seem to be lumps of uranium, gold foil, oil films, etc., and then extending the lessons to billiard balls, bars of gold, telescopes, observatories, libraries, and so on. Each of those things—which we feel so confident about because (we think!) we can not only see them but, unlike Macbeth feeling in vain for his dagger, can reach out and feel our hands touch them—are comparable to the bird that turns out to be a flock, the plane that turns out to be a squadron, and so on. If we could make ourselves tiny (even tinier than Alice was after she sprinkled the shrinking powder over her), we would see large objects invariably turn into *zillions of tiny bodies* rarely close enough to collide. We would also see that...

Nonexistent space distances each one from all the rest.

P.S. "What—or who!—is behind those bodies' movements?" is the question posed by the nuclear theory that led to the atomic destruction of Hiroshima and Nagasaki.

Nine. Think of 'light' as photons. Light isn't 'made up' of the infinitesimal bodies we call "photons." Photons, if they exist, remain photons the same way that stars, if they existed, would remain stars and not 'make up' galaxies at all. Photons can be collectively referred to by the shorthand cue, "light," the same way that zillions of protons, neutrons, and electrons can, in many cases, be conveniently, collectively, and fictitiously referred to as 'making up' stars or, in some other cases, the air we breathe. By reading enough books, you will learn that contemporary physicists have run into a monumental roadblock in their efforts to reach consensus on never-seen light. They need two absolutely incompatible models to help them conveniently predict the visible outcome of their 'experiments' with e.g., scintillation counters, silvered mirrors, diffraction gratings, fresnel lenses, etc., which, paradoxically, are all as never-seen and invisible as light is and all located in laboratories that are as much illusions as libraries! Only one of those two models makes literally good sense: the one which represents 'light' as zillions of separate, infinitesimal bodies. You must approach uses of the second model which translates "light" into "waves" with great caution. Dispel whatever nonsense users of the second model fall into by noting that *there are literally no waves as such.* What we mis-take as waves moving across the surface of the pond are illusions created when molecules which barely move sideways are squeezed upwards, then fall, are squeezed upwards, fall again, and so on. As for the rope 'illustrations,' if you are holding one end in your hand and the other is tied to a post, it is obvious that no part of it is going anywhere except up and down. So resist all the talk about light 'really!' being waves. Waves do not exist, there is no ether or space-time continuum to 'carry' them, and—even if there were—such a medium's properties would be totally self-cancelling. Read up on the solar-system model of the atom: when a planet-electron jumps from one energy orbit around the nucleus to another, it 'gives off' or 'absorbs' a photon. In his 1989 *The Emperor's New Mind*, Roger Penrose, some-time colleague of Stephen Hawking, pictured the orbit-jumping being so fast and furious that "A sixty-watt light bulb emits about 100 000 000 000 000 000 000 photons per second." (By searching enough books, you can find several authors to back you up on any of the answers you think are best for whatever question you are suddenly confronted with.) P.S. Invisible light has no color. Long ago, Newton warned that "If at any time I speak of light and rays as colored or endued with colours, I would be understood to speak not philosophically and properly, but grossly, and according to such conceptions as vulgar people in seeing all these experiments are apt to frame" (*Opticks*).

II. ETERNITY AND THE TIMES OF YOUR LIFE

I. The Myth of Distinct Disciplines. Or, "Introduction to Descartes." His *Meditations* made explicit what every? sociologist, anthropologist, historicist, and pantheist— i.e., every? groupist—hates to notice: that only individual humans utter and that each of their utterances expresses an individual-person'al opinion, not a social, cultural, historical, or divine one. Kant made the point a different way: every claim has an implicit preface that can be made explicit by adding "I think that..." That is not synonymous with "I believe that...," and I'd be lying if I led you to think I believe every sociologist, etc., hates to notice the obvious truth. (I think!) Cooley didn't.

That generalization applies here. That is, the above reflects my personal opinion that all opinions are personal ones. The coin's other side is that, in my personal opinion, there is no public opinion as such. Nor are there any collective bodies of knowledge: no science, no theology, no philosophy, and no psychology, astronomy, or astrology, and no history, sociology, or anthropology, etc. There are many private 'bodies' of human knowledge, 5.7 billion or one per citizen, minus the number of infants, etc., who have none. In *seeming* contrast to the stars in the public space above, all thoughts are private, found in humans' insides, which is where Kant said he found the awesome moral law. No matter what errors Descartes made, and he made many, we should be immensely grateful that God raised up such a prophet to pave the way for world democracy by finally clarifying the fact, for everyone with ears to hear and eyes to read, that every thought, however true or however false, is a private one belonging to one single citizen, the only type of citizen that exists. The implication is obvious: no good public opinion, only enough good personal ones.

Which is so obvious that it **appears** bewildering at first that there are people living today who think otherwise. Until we notice how it really **appears**, namely, that each individual's views are 'shaped' by society. Why did Moses think the earth was like a floating-on-water (not space) pancake? (Maybe that it rested on pillars? See *I Sam* 2:8.) Doesn't it seem easier to regard that as a myth taught by his society rather than as a truth revealed by God? Why did Aquinas, Moses' contemporary, believe that Aristotle's philosophy went well with revelation? Wasn't it because everyone who lived on the Gulf of Mexico sixty centuries ago was taught it in the public schools of that time? Why did those who read Moses and Aquinas believe God is male and created a man first and the wife second rather than the other way around? Wasn't it because they grew up in a society where men were the patriarchs and the women were taught to be subservient to their husbands? How many Hebrew children grew up as Buddhists, and how many children of the Yanomama in Brazil grow up as Hindus? Why do so many of today's 'scientific experts' regard the whole idea of God as bunk and so many 'spiritually oriented' view all stories and narratives, both scientific and religious, as equally valid—and equally mythical—attempts to eff about the ineffable ground of our being? Don't both types, who differ so radically from the natives living on the islands of Sumer and Babylon, appear to get their different ideas from the sub-culture societies they flock together with? Moses, Aquinas, and Aristotle didn't know these things because they had no sociology or anthropology. No one back in those days ever dreamed of calling her- or himself a "sociologist" or "anthropologist." Who back in those days did any calling in english? Isn't it obvious and apparent that society shapes us? Isn't that what our society teaches us?

But it's a myth. **No groups exist.** So society doesn't exist. How can we be shaped by what does not exist? "Society" is **shorthand** for many people who are alike in whatever ways any free-thinking 'definer' stipulates when s/he uses that 'symbol.' Look. It is individual parents, peers, teachers, pastors, media moguls, media celebrities, media foot-soldiers, etc., who individually exert the influence said to be exerted by "society." Use your own eyes to check the truth of this private opinion. Study the flight of birds and see if you see anything but birds. "Flock" is shorthand for many individuals acting in stipulated ways. Every alleged group—church, state, faculty, etc.—you study will, when viewed up close, turn out to be individuals, not a group. *It's the old difference between appearance and reality again.* Or between myth and science. Even without knowing that sociologists no more agree on what sociology is or should be than philosophers agree on what philosophy is or should

be, even without knowing the differences between
Cooley and Mead, Freeman and Mead, or Mead and
Mead, it is obvious each new learner personally learns
from individual teachers who each did her or his own
learning by using her or his own ears to hear what other
individuals said, own eyes to read what others wrote,
own mind to interpret either or both, own memory to
store up the body of not-yet-forgotten knowledge s/he
used to interpret whatever s/he heard or read, own will
to choose who s/he agreed and disagreed with on what,
and own lips or pen to teach with. Just as you are using
your own eyes to see these rows and rose of print, your
mind to interpret what you see, your memory to check
on whether your interpretations here are consistent with
your interpretations of what has preceded, and your will
to agree or disagree, not with society, but with me. Are
you me? Am I you? Confused about who did the writing
and who's doing the reading? Was Descartes wrong? Or
Kant?

Still, whoever wants to think *simultaneously* about
many individuals, as God must, must notice that we do
seem to mutually influence each other's thinking. As I
am trying to do re yours. Especially via words, words,
and more words. Thanks to libraries and the 'frozen'
words stored there, we can study the beliefs of thousands
of individuals and begin to take note of how the beliefs
of one are like the beliefs of some others, i.e., the ones
we then say are "from the same group." We can carry the
process further to form a God's-eye view of 'historical
progress' the way Hegel did, or a God's-eye view of the
changes in individuals' similar 'socio-economic' habits
as Marx did. True, such viewings attend to distinctive

samenesses in abstraction from numerous other and different distinctive samenesses the way the musically-trained selectively attend to distinct 'themes' weaving through a Bach fugue, but we would be poorer in part if we were ignorant of the important and distinctive samenesses in the diverse, 24-hrs/day background muzaks—words, words, and more words—that make up part of what we call the "diverse cultures" inhabited by unique individual humans. *The Social Construction of Reality* (Berger and Luckmann) is valuable meditation-material for this. So long as you change "social" to "personal."

Whoever aspires to become a truth-believing scientist must reject two errors which our society! teaches us: the Myth of Distinct Disciplines and the Myth of Science's Superiority. Our whole system of education* from beginning to end is organized on the premise that there are independent fields where truth can be learned separately from what other fields teach, and that 'science' is the name for a superior kind of knowledge known only by special experts named 'scientists.' So entrenched are these myths, that those who want respect pass off their field as 'science,' a product of that superior path to reliable knowledge, the 'scientific' method (see how many psychology, economics, even management!, texts have chapters on science and its superior method), and dismiss internal disagreements on basic principles with the lame "Oh, our 'science' is still young" excuse! (*All useful shorthand.)

True, there is a solid core of truth to the Twin Myths. Galileo was more right about how the heavens go than the so-called philosophers and theologians who hounded him. Kant and Lyell were more correct about the origin of our planet than *Genesis'* author, and Darwin had a better model to help understand biology than Augustine. Freud knew in far more detail than the Greeks how hard it is to "know thyself," and Kelly was smarter than either in recognizing that all of us use the same 'scientific' method. True, the deterministic thermodynamics espoused by Einstein wasn't the whole truth, as Bohr insisted, and Bohr's complementarity was only a useful fiction, as Einstein insisted, but both knew more even than John Dalton. Modern physics is superior to that of the pre-moderns, a claim proven by the results we refer to with the umbrella-term, "technology": for instance, by the word-processors that allow us writers to produce our own texts and revise them without troubling a secretary, the laser printers that churn out millions of times more machine-scripts than whole armies of medieval copyists could have produced manu-scripts, the telephones which are far more reliable than telepathy, etc. On and on go lists of technological miracles that go far beyond Francis Bacon's wildest forecasts. But...

II. A third, God-taught myth: naive realism. Education, even at MIT and Harvard, is dominated by naive realism, an outlook that is pre-scientific. The same, gigantic mass of 'facts' that proves the superiority of the moderns' over the ancients' physics also proves that those descriptions of technology's miracles are naive. There are no word processors, no computers, no laser printers, no hands, no phones, and so on. No laboratories with accelerators to hurry particles or bubble chambers to detect them, no libraries with books in them to explain what "SSC" and "top quark" refer to. Theories about bodies are as unprovable in 1995 as Kant realized they were 200 years ago. And, in Popper's terms, as unfalsifiable. That is why Descartes who, in the 1600's, believed bodies do exist and Berkeley who, in the 1700's, believed they don't both failed to convince readers they had proven their opposed conclusions.

What is "naive realism" shorthand for? For one third of our early commonsense belief-system, which third rests on two beliefs: that there exist physical bodies that get along without us and that the things we sense (see, hear, etc.) are those physical bodies themselves. The evidence is so over-whelmingly inconsistent with *the combination* of those beliefs that, when Einstein was asked to write a word or two for the Schilpp volume on Bertrand Russell, he said that naive realism is easy to get over (not true!) and applauded the way Russell summed up the present situation in his (Russell's) *An Inquiry into Meaning and Truth*. He cited the latter's words.

> We all start from "naive realism," i.e., the doctrine that things are what they seem. We think grass is green, that stones are hard, and that snow is cold. But physics assures us that the greenness of grass, the hardness of stones, and the coldness of snow are not the greenness, hardness, and coldness that we know in our experience, but something very different. The observer, when he seems to himself to be observing a stone, is really, *if physics is to be believed*, observing the *effects* of the stone upon himself. Thus science seems to be at war with itself; when it most means to be objective, it finds itself plunged into subjectivity against its will. Naive realism leads to physics, and physics, if true, shows that naive realism is false. Therefore naive realism, if true, is false; therefore it

is false. (*An Inquiry Into Meaning and Truth*, Intro.; emphases added.)

Understanding Russell is really not at all difficult. It's believing him that is. Back to your picture of yourself looking up from the ground at the starry heavens above. Add a swarm of mosquitoes to that picture *which is your step-ladder* to the scientific discoveries which Descartes, Berkeley, Hume, Kant, Russell, Einstein, and the other white, male, European giants of modern thought have made. Next, ask: is there anything which the ground beneath your feet, stars over your head, mosquitoes buzzing around you, and other people have in common? Yes, they are all 'without' or on your out-side, whereas the awe you feel at the so-distant stars and the awe you feel when you contemplate the so-close moral law are both 'within' or on your in-side where Kant felt the moral law itself was. The key to clear and distinct thinking is **your skin**: it divides any hypothesized causes on your out-side from every sensed effect on your in-side. (An important footnote is that all 5,699,999,000 of us others, both <u>our</u> out sides and <u>our</u> in sides, are on <u>your</u> out one. Compare the in side vs the out side of your skin with the left vs the right side of a line drawn on a slate.) Russell's and Einstein's meaning is clear. Things you see and hear seem to be on the out side of your skin but are really, as an honest and unequivocal admission of sound's and light's finite speed proves, sensible **effects** which are produced on your skin's in side by whatever unseen **causes** exist on your skin's out side. Then there's your brain...

So important are the physics of sound and light that it is worth a few moments to review them from another angle. First, do as the clever line suggests and stop the world merry-go-round the way you would to 'get off.' Freeze everything. Make every single thing dead in its tracks. Return earth to the state Galileo's enemies thought it never left, imagine the distant stars no longer fleeing, and fill the empty space between stars and earth with zillions of stopped photons. Wrap the moon and earth with blankets of vibrationless atoms referred to as "atmosphere" for short. (The 8-10-93 *N.Y. Times* reported that the moon's thin atmosphere is estimated to consist of as many as 10 million atoms per cubic centimeter, that is, only about one trillionth as many as earth's.) Finally, add 5.7 billion still humans, separated from each other by space full of immobile light photons and atmospheric atoms. If ever the world and its occupants were thus frozen, your 'world' would be pitch dark, for no light would reach your eyes, and dead silent, for no vibrations would reach your ears. Nor would any mosquito land on your skin to cause an itch. Inside you.

The 'case' is airtight. Anyone who is able to count the seconds between a flash of lightning and a rumble of thunder has proof that air vibrations take time to travel. As for light, Olaus Roemer nailed down its finite velocity in 1675, a mere quarter of a century after Descartes died; three centuries after Roemer, Einstein's untrue but useful principle—nothing goes faster than light—has become the very cornerstone of physics. No wonder Einstein described Russell's way of putting physics' stunning conclusion into such stunning prose as "masterful," adding that it even helped him grasp the true significance of Berkeley and Hume. Agree or not, you do at least understand, do you not? The point is this: **if you agree with the physics**, then it follows that you've never sensed the grass, stone, or snow on your out side, but only the **effects** produced—like the mosquito's itch—on your in side by those never-seen, at-best-hypothesized **causes** on your out side. (Keep pretending for now that you have skin.) It also follows from contemporary physics that this is not a book that you see, but part of the **effect** of never-seen light bouncing off its pages and flying right into your eyes, just the same way that it's never us that you hear, but only **effects** caused by or correlated with the unheard air-molecule vibrations passing from vocal cords, through the atmosphere, to your eardrums.

III. Switchable mindsets and inconsistency. (***Mark this as a crucial section.) One of the things you will notice—if you are reading carefully—is that there are dozens of literal contradictions in these pages which are not pages. The reason is simple: *it is impossible to guide you step by step to a radically new way of viewing everything without beginning where we all do, theoretically, which is with the commonsense theory that we learn before we ever learn what learning is.* That is why, even after pointing out that, say, words or groups do not exist, I switch back and forth in order to build a bridge from part of one view to part of the other, to show how to translate from one form of shorthand to another. We begin life with no theory. Around the age of five or six, we begin our moral life by using our commonsense theory and its naive-realist component. We must then begin our unique climb from naive realism to—we hope—higher truths by choosing parts of it over others. Everyone, both Platos and Einsteins, must choose individually. And with care, lest what was meant to be a climb to wisdom become a descent to folly. Therefore...

As newer ideas are proposed in successive re-meditations, you will have to re-read earlier pages in a new way. For instance, if you 'followed' the first two chapters, you will have learned that I do not believe what is implied by the Preface. There are no men's or women's voices. Perry Como's certainly isn't 'stored' in a million different places, nor is a woman's voice lurking in a micro-chip at school, just waiting to talk to us. As for Hawking...

Berkeley faced and partly solved this challenge three centuries ago in his *Principles*. But he made mistakes, and one was suggesting that the learned do not think the way laypeople do. **All of us revert to naive realism** the instant our attention to rival theories relaxes as we turn to our usual, everyday decisions. And—unless we suffer senility—our habitual use of it will keep it not only fresh in mind but partly on-stage even when we switch to our 'professed' or 'professional' alternative! But!!! Just as our everyday talk about the sun rising and the sky being blue does not make such talk true and is no excuse for physics texts to offer such antique physics as an option, so the everyday assumptions that larger-than-subatom-sized bodies exist and that we can sense them do not make such naive beliefs true and are no excuse for most text-book authors to continue writing as if they are. Especially when naive layfolk are vulnerable to the myth about physics being more certain than theology. Neither physics nor theology exist, only the private opinions of individual citizens, opinions no better than the evidence and logic backing them up, opinions no better because a million naked emperors espouse them. That's my personal opinion. P.S. Meditate a few minutes on the instant mindset-switching spies and undercover cops must do.

IV. Time is imaginary. The last chapter or re-meditation centered on pretending that space is a container for everything that exists. Existing things change, and we need some way to keep our thoughts straight about those changings. Your present efforts to learn about quintalism (that is a handy shorthand for the theory built on a claim that only five types of things exist and change) are part of a lifetime of efforts that you'll exert. In order to gain the kind of self-knowledge the Greeks advised, it is essential to begin—unless you are already in the habit—paying as much attention to time as you do to space. (Your now will be later in time than my 5-30-95, and you'll have to guess what the real I am doing during your right-now.) Unless you are different from the rest of us on your out side whose constantly growing bodies of personally-acquired knowledge are, like yours, located on our in sides (but your out side), then your store of memories is constantly increasing as you travel from womb to tomb, crib to coffin, nether world to after life, or what have you. ("What **do** we have?" is the $64-dollar question. Or was, before inflation.) The more times you re-read and re-flect on these chapters, the more times your meditations become re-meditations, the more acutely aware you should become of the fact that a dateable-by-time dimension is as much part of your experience as a locatable-in-space one. Even though time is just as imaginary as space.

Demo Let your day-by-day learning process become the key for learning about time and about which of the things on your in side are most important. Without turning your whole body around, look behind you and make a mental note of what you see. Now that you are looking back up front here, try to recall what you saw. Was it your past, which people will tell you is 'behind you'? Turn the pages back(ward) to the Preface that you'll find before this chapter, this much of which you have read after reading the Preface before it. As you do, notice that you can turn pages back the way you turn your clock back, but you cannot turn time back. That is, if you have already read the Before-face, your next reading will be a re-reading that can only take place sometime in the future which is still before you, that is, at a point in time ahead of the point called "now," which point lay ahead of the point in time when your first reading took place back in your past, which past is where your reading of the "now" earlier in this sentence is now located, time-wise. As you read on and on—or even on and back—in this book (or is it on and on—but never back—in the future?), that is, as you scan ever-new rows and rose which are old and co-existed in the past before you ever began to read them (or would have, if books existed), that is, as you go on and on while sitting still, always looking ahead of you in the present, now at this (row) and now at this (one), you are constantly experiencing and, unless you do not retain what you are learning, constantly finding (or re-finding) out how much talk (thoughts?) about space and time overlap. Even though neither exists. **End**

It was Bergson's discussion about 'spatializing time' that made me superconscious, far back in my past, of the fact that we can draw a single line on a page and then use it with equal ease to represent either space- or time-dimensions. It serves equally well as an aid to cosmic geography or to cosmic history, both of which every well-educated citizen today should have at least a rough picture of. (Experts will rightly be appalled at **the bad history injected earlier in this chapter**, errors no one who has not personally learned enough history can identify, no matter how advanced her or his 'society' or 'culture' may be.) We must begin with facts, and the fact is that a line can be a symbol for whatever we make it a symbol of. Put two dots on a piece of paper, label them 0 & 5, and draw *the shortest line!* you can between them. Divide it into 5 equal segments with four markers, 1 to 4. Now note: **0** can stand equally well for the moment of the Big Bang, the planet earth, the femto-instant before you began to exist, or New York City; **5** can represent equally well the year 1995 A.D., the sun, the fifth anniversary of your existence, and Los Angeles; and **the line** can easily symbolize the duration of this Burst, the amount of empty space between earth and sun, your first five years of being, or the distance between NYC and LA. Do you at least understand the thoughts that just came to you. Even if you disagree?

Here, finally, is the way to read physics: with one eye on the common moral sense we rely on in our dealings with other people. Kant taught this when he wrote one critique to show that scientific cockiness is naive and a second to tell us why, for example, we should put expressing compunction ahead of being able to discuss the metaphysics of it. The enormous appeal of Marx's idea that changing the world is more important than just contemplating it comes from its link with our common moral sense. James based not only his life but many of his theoretical positions on it. Now notice: **All thinking about life and life's purpose hinges around our beliefs about time and change.** Think of your ideas of pleasure and guilt, merit and blame, memory, confident knowledge, and expectation. When was the last time you went out of your way to please another? When was the last time you were unkind? If you were reading an article in *Readers Digest*, would you think such questions made fairly good sense? Do they make sense within the context of your physics and its theory about time? If not, then you are a theory-schizophrenic. You are like theologians who take matter on faith but think physics is different from theology, sociologists who mutually disprove each other's claims to science, evolutionists who pontificate as if their speculations about bodies—and life?!—in the past can evade uncertainty about bodies' existence in the present, etc. Remember that

...all knowledge and all time-bound thought works the same way. For instance, did you read the last paragraph while standing or standing on your head, sitting or lying down, or in some other position? STOP. How can you possibly learn the answer to that question? Can you look into the past to see what you were doing while you were reading? The universe is presently full of presently-existing things. There is no room in it for the past. So, in which direction would you look to see it? Unless you stop here!, you are going to be using up some of your future trying to answer that question. Where is your future?

The whole universe is presently full of presently-existing things. There is no room in it for the future. Applied... If you did something kind for someone recently but are not doing it now, then it is, we say, 'part of the (no-longer-existing) past,' and if you haven't yet been thanked for it but hope to be, it will have to be sometime, as we say, 'in the (not-yet existing) future.' Keep the preceding thoughts in mind when you go to the library to begin exploring all the wild theories on time in it. Sometime in the future, of course. Unless you already read them in the past.

Most thinkers either propose truly bizarre notions about time or else rely heavily on the everyday equivocations demonstrated in the earlier "Demo" you can re-read later. But all began with the same everyday good-sense that makes all of us laugh at Zeno's time-paradoxes, at least until we get serious about time. Repeat: good sense is far and away our best guide in evaluating the dozens upon dozens of theories that have been produced, both by Zeno and Aristotle before the time Augustine noted how confidently he could talk about time except during the times when he was being asked "What is time?", and after his time by Newton, Kant, and dozens of others who've tried their hand at the question whose trickiness Augustine described so memorably. Especially in distilling the truth from the science-fiction offered to non-experts ever since Einstein learned some simplifying tricks to use in calculating the exact dimensions of non-existent space between bodies and the exact dimensions of non-existent duration-times in the equable flow of non-existent time-duration. Because Einstein's theories have wreaked havoc with thousands of people's good sense, take a few moments to recall what's obviously plain commonsense.

First, were you alive when you read the question re your *Readers Digest* reading? Were you reading, sitting (or whatever), *and* living *at the very same time*? Before you answer, see if you understand the questions. Einstein got a letter from a young woman once: "I probably would have written to you ages ago," she wrote, "only I was not aware you were still alive. I am not interested in history, and I thought that you had lived in the eighteenth century. I must have been mixing you up with Sir Isaac Newton or someone." To which Einstein replied: "Thank you for your letter of July 10th. I have to apologize to you that I am still among the living. There will be a remedy for this, however." Then he got down to the business of answering her question about the meaning of curved space: "Be not worried about 'curved space.' You will understand at a later time that for it this status is the easiest it could possibly have. Used in the right sense the word 'curved' has not exactly the same meaning as in everyday language." (Do you know whether I am making up this letter or not?) Can you be alive, hold your breath, *and* read the above *at the same time*? Can you be not-dead, not-breathe, *and* not not-read? *Simultaneously*?

If you re-view the above paragraph, you will find certain terms which, there, in that paragraph, mean the same thing. I know, because I am the one who, when I reread it, see that I *mean* them to convey ("meaning" is got by taking the verb and adding "ing") or *intend* you to think ("intention" converts the verb into the noun the same way "meaning" does) the same thought. They are "when," "at the very same time," "at the same time," and "simultaneously." In the same Schilpp essay, Einstein criticized the 'fear of metaphysics' which Russell, like many of his contemporaries, seemed to display until the very last chapter of *An Inquiry into...* Einstein's final comment was "The only thing to which I take exception there is the bad intellectual conscience which shines through between the lines"! To me, that sounds far more damning even than what James wrote to Peirce: "I am *a*-logical, if not illogical, and glad to be so when I find Bertie Russell trying to excogitate what true knowledge means, in the absence of any concrete universe surrounding the knower and the known. Ass!" (Are you sure I'm not making up this letter, too?) But, in the one book which he wrote to explain to layfolk what he was proposing by *Relativity: the Special and General Theory*, Einstein committed the same 'postivist'-inspired sin that he accused Russell of. It hinged around the concept named "simultaneity."

> The concept does not exist for the physicist until he has the possibility of discovering whether or not it is fulfilled in an actual case. We thus require a definition of simultaneity such that this definition supplies us with the method by means of which, in the present case, he can decide by experiment whether or not both the lightning strokes occurred simultaneously. At long as this requirement is not satisfied, I allow myself to be deceived as a physicist (and of course the same applies if I am not a physicist), when I imagine that I am able to attach a meaning to the statement of simultaneity. (I would ask the reader not to proceed farther until he is fully convinced on this point.) After thinking... [From ch. 8, "On the Concept of Time in Physics"]

Believe it or not, Einstein later referred to this **crucial** premise in his relativity theory as "nonsense'! (See W.Heisenberg, *Physics and Beyond*, p.63, and L. Gilder, *The Age of Entanglement*, p.86.)

The radical disagreements among physicists when they are asked "What is a space-time continuum?" were brought to my attention by an anthology, *Readings in the Philosophy of Nature* (H.Koren, ed., 1958) which reprinted a long essay by M.Capek. In it, he reported on Einstein's own protests against mis-interpretations. And then went on to say that the trouble with "Where is Andromeda nebula *now*?" is that final word. "There are, as Eddington used to say, no 'world-wide instants'; or, in the words of A.A.Robb, 'an instant cannot be in two places at once.' *My present instant is here and nowhere else*" (p.301). The truth is that there are no instants of any kind anywhere. Only things that exist exist, and all of them are persons (not you), the thoughts they understand (you do not understand any), what they sense (read no more because you can't see these rows and rose anyway), memory-images of what they've sensed (you've sensed nothing), or subatoms (these are the only truly real things). Some of the deepest mysteries here come from geometry. Remember the three imaginary lines meeting in your midriff? I was kidding. They are real. But they have only one dimension apiece: one is front & back, one is right & left, and one is up & down. Before you do real geometry, you must add more parallel lines. Around the first, add an infinite number parallel to it, as many as you can squeeze into infinite space. If you can find any extra space, add just as many parallels to the second. Ditto for the third. This will insure that you have three point**s** in every point! where parallels to the original lines intersect. The mystery that results is that the map-line representing the distance from NYC to LA has exactly as many points as the real distance: an infinite number. Points, Euclid held, have no dimensions, otherwise points would be lines, surfaces, or solids, not points. To get the others, you need an infinity of points. If you have any room left over, add the time-line's points to get your 4-D space-time continuum. Acc to *Mathematics for the General Reader,* by E.C.Titchmarsh, who held the Savilian chair at Oxford, this yields...

> ...a four-dimensional Cartesian geometry. It is impossible to visualize it, but as a mathematical system it is not much more difficult to handle than three-dimensional geometry. In fact we can introduce any number of dimensions in the same way. (Ch.V)

No wonder M.Kline declared in *Mathematics and the Search for Knowledge* that "the greatest science fiction stories are in the science of physics" (ch.VI on gravity)! Prove (now) that you were not created, memories and all, just ten minutes ago.

3. YOUR LIFE, YOUR 'WORLD,' AND CONVERSIONS

Naturally, I cite Titchmarsh for one reason. (I think!) He knows what he's talking about, and his view is a piece that fits an area of the (my) grand jigsaw puzzle. I try to find authorities for each claim I make. Here is another example. It is copied from the forward of J.Brown's and P.Davies' (editors) *The Ghost in the Atom*:

> A final thought and a note of caution; when we commissioned the interviews, several of our contributors (who shall remain nameless!) expressed the view that there is now no real doubt over how quantum theory should be interpreted. At the very least, we hope this book will show that there is little justification for such complacency. (1986)

P.S. If a physics teacher says space is curved or the universe is finite-but-unbounded and begins to claim such non-euclidean fiction is true by asking you to pretend the curved lines on a 3-D doorknob or horse-saddle are as straight as Euclid's 2-D ones, remind them that Einstein confessed in writing that "curved" in curved space "has not exactly the same meaning as in everyday language." Even kids can understand that there are two routes from NYC to LA: the curved one the crow uses and which is impossible to put onto a flat map of the USA, and the straight one only moles use. P.P.S. It's non-euclideans' "straight" that throws us the curve. P.P.P.S. Which body moves? Does the plane curve around from NYC to LA as it might seem from one 'stationary' satellite, or does LA come to the plane as it would seem from a different 'stationary' satellite? Zeno said that, since nothing is ever in more than one place at a time, and since there is never more than one time at a time, nothing moves, so motion is an illusion. But is that belief practical? What's practical? End of P.S.

V. "Eternity" names a concept we create. We begin with before-and-after-before-and-after, etc., events we have personal memories of. E.g., I say "Stand," X stands, I ask "Why did you stand?", X says "Because you told me to," I say "Lie down, face on the floor," X doesn't, I ask "Why didn't you?", X says "I didn't want to," etc. We mentally line those *event-memories* up, with earlier ones to the left! of later ones (if our reading habits run left to right), so that we can mentally situate each in relation to the others. (For laughs, we can scramble the order.) We fill in our memory-gaps with inferred goings-on (as Hume noted), then imagine an invisible river of *time* whose flow is synchronous with the events. **Artificial** time-*measuring* began with efforts to find other uniform *movements* besides **nature's** day-ly sunrise and year-ly seasons. Lastly, we extend the invisible event-containing time-line endlessly in both directions, just as we extended the invisible body-containing space endlessly in all directions. By making us who view everything from the middle of space, with what amounts to a T.Nagel-like *View From Nowhere*, so dependent upon invisible light's visible effects as clues to stars that are trillions of miles away and to events that occurred billions of years ago, God has set limits on the things we can claim to have an 'empirical' basis for. John Locke said we know all we need to know, and then Socrates-like explained why being undogmatic about what we don't know is so vital for toleration toward others who think they know better.

A. Preface-2. After graciously reading a précis of the theory being expanded-upon here, an acquaintance said that it made him think of "an intellectual autobiography, first and foremost." The only way to explain why he disagreed with this or that conclusion, he added, would be to write an account of his own intellectual odyssey. Life is busy, and our discussion went no further. But his perceptive observation captured every person's situation. All of us carry, inside, the story of his or her life to the present. That story would be the history of two creations. One, the creation of the theoretical mindset we use to interpret each day's worth of our new experiences, including our theories about others' mindsets. Two, the creation of the habits we shorthand as "our moral character," a creation utterly dependent on the former, which fact explains why animals are so utterly devoid of moral character.

Picture your theoretical mindset as a steady-state model of the outer world emerging very gradually from your fast-moving stream of sense experience. The framework of that theoretical mindset gets stronger and more inflexible as you get older, which makes large conversions less likely. Not impossible, though. Just less likely. Small conversions—changes—are constant. You are constantly adding new bits of memory and information to your inner geography and history: new info about things you're already acquainted with, new info about things you knew nothing about. You link together things you formerly distinguished, like the Morning and Evening Star. You unlink what you've been in the habit of smooshing together, like the girl in So. Africa who learned that Newton and Einstein were separate persons to be marked separately on her world-history time-line. You may shift entire clusters of beliefs from "true" to "false," as when you decide "astrology" is pseudo-science since its basic premise-belief is about constellations which, you discover, do not exist.

This remediation deals chiefly with converting from one grand view of everything to another. This type of conversion involves wholesale or general decisions about what exists, about what goes in your model.

B. Understanding BIG thoughts. Whoever can read and understand this can also write her/his own life-story and include everything in it. Everything in general. Start with a test: see which of the following makes sense to you. "Seventy is the sum of our years, or eighty, if we are strong" and "From one point of view, it would have made very little difference to the universe if I had never been born, but from another point of view, the nonexistence of the universe would have made no difference if I had never been born." Which of those passages makes more sense to you? Everything that follows depends on how you answer the next question. "What does 'makes sense' mean?"

What *does* it mean??? Before you can figure out which makes more, you have to know what makes some. That makes sense, no? And you have to know the answer to "What does 'makes sense' mean?" in order to test yourself. After all, you cannot test yourself till you know the instructions. That, too, makes sense, no? As simple as such questions seem, they can be viewed as the issues most debated during this twentieth and greatest of centuries. You will have to use the library to learn about all the details. Here there is room only for one person's conclusions. First, "See which of the following makes sense" often means simply, "See which you can understand." It can also mean "Which do you agree with, i.e., which do you think is true?" I presume that, like me, you can understand both meanings. If you cannot, you'll be unable to say whether or not you agree with anything. (Do you reely kniht that pirots kerulize elactically? Be honest.) The distinction helps to explain why we often understand very well, indeed, what someone else says, but still insist that what they are saying makes no sense at all. Now test yourself. See which of the two quotes (maybe both?) makes sense to you. In both senses.

"Seventy is the sum of our years, or eighty if we are strong" is from Psalm 90, and people have been reading it in their prayers for centuries, which means we are not so different from them after all. Everyone is able to understand that line from the ancient psalm, but not one person can do it on the day s/he is born. Notice, though. The end of that sentence, if it is true, requires a change in the first half. The opening must be qualified to read: "Everyone old enough to have learned the basic common-sense theory and the 'english' set of cues & clues to it is able…" Still, being able to understand something does not mean that a person actually does it. No one knows anything they have never learned. So, even though you and I both understand the *Genesis* story about God creating the universe in six days and resting on the seventh, as well as the theory that the universe began with a Big Bang about fifteen billion years ago, no one cut off from the outside world the way the older Tasaday (reportedly?) were, will in fact know either the Big Week or the Big Bang theory. And no human learner will be able to think a thought big enough to compare both of them with the available evidence who does not first learn both rival theories. And no one will be able to compare that 'comparing' thought with what Plato wrote in his *Theatetus* to show that, in order to grasp the difference* between seeing colors we can't hear and hearing sounds we can't see, we need a third ability (a mind?) enabling us to 'see' and compare both simultaneously, until s/he sees how comparing any two things requires an ability to know the two things compared and to then compare each with still other items referred to as "evidence." (*The same power is needed to see that both are also alike, otherwise they'd not both be called "sensing.") And it won't be till later, after countless such thoughts, that we can begin to appreciate what a vast amount of information one learner can learn to cope with. Think, for instance, of what's in the library: books with opinions offered by thousands of individuals, all of whom work with a whole theoretical mindset. Then look into books on the history of western thought and meditate on how many other individual thinkers' grand unified views of everything have to be learned by each historian and inserted into his or her own grand unified view of everything. No one who has not lived long enough to be capable of such grand-theory-of-everything thoughts can fathom the monumental achievements of Hegel, Frederick Copleston SJ, or John Passmore, all of whom had to gradually learn enuf, personally!, and individually!, to have his big, bigger, and biggest thoughts comparing dozens upon dozens of partly different-and-partly-similar intellectual biographies and their many facets. For an idea of what a pinnacle 'vision' can seem like, read Diotima's description of the successful learner's vision of Beauty Itself (in Plato's *Symposium*). David Hume, surprisingly, once had a big enough thought about big thinkers' mastery of big thoughts and captured the nature of such **miraculous!** experiences in memorable prose:

> Nothing is more admirable than the readiness with which the imagination suggests its ideas, and presents them at the very instant in which they become necessary or useful. The fancy runs from one end of the universe to the other, in collecting those ideas which belong to any subject. One would think the whole intellectual world of ideas was at once subjected to our view, and that we did nothing but pick out such as were most proper for our purpose. There may not,

however, be any present, beside those very ideas, that are thus collected by a kind of magical faculty in the soul which... is however inexplicable by the utmost efforts of human understanding. (*Treatise* I:I:VII)

As you read *Re-Meditations*, the question is whether you'll grasp the sense it makes.

C. Pluralism. Because there are just too many individuals with their billion-faceted mindsets for us to deal with individually the way God must, it was necessary to devise a way for us to think-together many things at once. Think-together is part of what "con-cept" must have originally been a metaphor for. When we think many things together, we often use verbal 'shorthand' in trying to help others 'get' what we are thinking. For instance, what Hume refers to in the first line would be quite misleading if taken one way. There is no "*THE!* imagination." There are as many imaginations as there are humans able to imagine. That is, to entertain thoughts. And each person, with a separate imagination, creates a personal inner model. Note that Hume does not say that we know the world that is on our out side. We know ideas on our in side. A whole 'world' of them. And each person has her/his own 'world.' There are enough belief-systems to go around, so we each get our own.

And none is wholly like that of any other, the proof of which is abundant, as anyone familiar with the library or the evening knews nose: each person is as apt to disagree as to agree with any other person at any given moment on any given topic. Each of us is learning at every waking moment, and our waking moments are, however much alike, so very different, an obvious fact for those in the habit of attending to real, day-by-day, hour-by-hour experiences, the only kind that exist. Alas, we seldom pay enough attention to real facts. <u>Notice.</u> Even if your calendar reads the same as it did earlier, your watch will tell you it's later, and much has changed since then. RFR used that in yesterday's sermon. In an average hour in the US, 3 are murdered, 84 die of heart disease, 138 couples decide to divorce, and 175 women decide to abort. He got those figures from a book in the library. In an average hour, your body adds 12 billion new cells, about 10 billion of which are red blood cells. I got those from a book. Nothing like these figures were available in Descartes' day, but he provided the perfect framework for both the figures and for the thoughts you are having of them as you continue scanning these rows and rose. Whether or not you question those figures, you do understand them, right? Were you capable of understanding these thoughts when you were still in your crib? Did you not first have to learn about life and death, different kinds of death, divorce and marriage and the words "till death do us part," cells, and erythrocytes, in the time-period between back then and right now? And learn what "learn" means, what "continue" means, what "scan" means, what "rose" means, etc.? Incidentally, what does "rose" mean? Is it singular or plural? A noun or a verb in the past tense? Is "rose" a word or four letters? One thing, many things, one group 'made up of' many things, or what? Does the dictionary have a separate section to tell you the answers to those questions which will repeat themselves when you look up "rose" in another section? No, the instructions for interpreting dictionaries are learned in everyday life, which is also where we learn to distinguish books from drums, reading from drumming, written language from musical notation, and so on. Do a check. Are you reading or drumming? Do you need a book to tell you? Are you breathing air, too? Air? Did you learn yet that, in ordinary air, "each molecule collides with some other molecule about 3000 million times every second and travels an average distance of about 1/160000 inch between successive collisions"? J.Jeans' *The Universe Around Us* says so, or at least that's what E.Kasner and J.Newman said in *Mathematics and the Imagination*. Did you know the last two facts before? What book did you learn them from? From this one? Is this a book? Are you scanning musical notation or written words? Or just seeing shaped black figures against a white background? Are there any thoughts coming to you as you continue scanning? Is there any order to them? Is the order reasonable enuf that, like Hobbes, you'd describe it as "a train of thoughts"? See now if you can understand, from the many theses which are being brought to your notice in conjunction with these cues and clues, how and why **whatever learning any human has done can be fitted into her or his own life story**? It can, if that life story includes a record of every true fact as well as of every error learned. And, with that fact as background, you can understand why Socrates advised that each person examine closely each bit of information s/he has gullibly gotten used to believing without question, why Descartes re-advised the same thing, why—with all the background 'noise' called "today's culture"—it is even more important than ever for those citizens who prefer to take a hand in hiring the people whose legally-reached decisions they agree to follow. <u>Notice.</u> With all that as background, i.e., as context, you will find that it makes good sense to combine two things we normally oppose to each other. Normally, we think it makes sense to ask people "Is your knowledge of that fact first- or second-hand?" It makes sense to ask "Did you see him stab her or did X tell you— say to you—that he stabbed her?" But no one can know what X says unless s/he knows first-hand that X exists, what X said, etc. What people know 'second-hand,' they don't know for sure unless they know many other things for sure. Anyone who hasn't personally observed Jupiter's moons and done the subsequent math Olaus Roemer did but believes that "It's been proven scientifically that light takes time to travel" takes many things on faith, not one. S/he takes it on faith that (if it exists) light travels at a finite speed, s/he takes it on faith that, e.g., Roemer saw things and did a great deal of logically valid reasoning to arrive at the truth expressed by "Light travels at a finite speed," etc. Do you accept the latest word that light goes exactly 299,792,458 meters/second? I take 'their' word on thousands of things. If what they say is consistent with everything else.

Why call this section "pluralism"? To underline the idea that generalizations, e.g., about 'the imagination,' are shorthand for thoughts about many particulars. In the words of James, "**No one sees farther into a generalization than his own knowledge of details extends.**" James' thought-system has been given many names. Three of them are naturalism, pragmatism, and radical empiricism. But, in view of his vocal opposition to monism and his insistence on realities in the plural, it is also called "pluralism." "A Pluralistic Universe" was the title of his final set of public lectures, and "A Pluralistic

Mystic" was the title of the last article he polished for publication, and it is hard to think of a better name for him than that, even though he used it for Paul Blood, a barely-known thinker whose conversion from a kind of pantheist monism to a dogged pluralism it was James' dying wish to see publicized. (That's dramatic license, but only slightly.) What does it mean here?

You must quit thinking that thoughts float about in splendid isolation. Every thought is someone's thought, and every thinker is a unique thinker. Each person's thoughts have as their context the rest of that individual's beliefs, and each thinker knows others only '<u>through</u>' her or his own private thoughts.

Those are clues to my thoughts. Did you just get thoughts about mine? Whatever thoughts you had were 1/5.7 billionth of the thoughts God was keeping track of. Namely, yours. It's time for you to notice with full force what is utterly obvious: every thought that's ever come to you—about astrologers, Einstein, Newton, James, Descartes, pluralism, etc.—has been *a thought of yours*, a thought accompanied by a network of sensory-expectancies, proposed to a mental giant (you!). These 'word' cues and clues re-mind you of what you already know, prompt you to zoom in and add a detail here or there or to change a detail here or there, invite you to re-label an old belief (e.g., about brains, gravity, mental illnesses, etc.) as "a useful(?) fiction" or to reinstate a previously-discarded one (as happens when people recover a belief in God), etc. Conclusion-thesis: each person knows only as much as s/he has learned up to the present and has not forgotten. A generalization-detail: **YOU know only as much as YOU have learned up to the present and have not forgotten.**

D. Mindset-conversions. The best book to read before you go farther is the second of James' masterpieces, the one he actually titled *The Varieties of Religious Experience*, the one he ought to have titled The Varieties of (Human) Experience. His ideas on the divided self and the unification-process or conversion apply in a broad way to one of the chief features of all 'scientific inquiry,' namely, the urge to find a way of overcoming a sense that "something's wrong." Whether with how we are living (James' focus there) or with what we believe (here). Descartes' conversion away from "our senses give us all our data" naive-realism, Kepler's conversion from circles to ellipses, Newton's conversion to a unified earth-and-sky science, Russell's conversion back from his conversion to idealism: they are all covered by what James wrote. Your goal is a coherent belief system that has room for everything, a belief system that is **an inner cosmic history of doings represented in a cosmic geography**.

The radical mindset-conversion Descartes underwent must be a historical milestone for anyone whose goal is a scientific GUTE or **g**rand **u**nifying **t**heory of **e**verything. He offered a radically simplified way of viewing everything. In part, his move can be viewed as a further step in the everyday simplification needed to play the game of Twenty Questions. To play that game, we must be able to lump existing things into four types: minerals, vegetables, animals, and humans. Rocks, beds, toys, machines, computers, etc., are mineral bodies with no sensations, no feelings, and no opinions. Other things like plants, with no sensations, no feelings, and no opinions, can take in nourishment, grow, and reproduce, while still other things not only do the latter but have sensations and feelings as well. Finally, there are we humans who express opinions that hurt others' feelings and who may burn others at the stake, even fight wars, because of differences in our utterly invisible opinions. Descartes said, "No, there are only two kinds of things: dead bodies, and conscious spirits." Or, extended nonpersons, and nonbodily persons. Or minerals, and persons who are not animals at all. He began with familiar ideas. Haven't people always believed that there are two kinds of things in the universe: seen and unseen? Seen ones have shape and size, are three-dimensional and tangible. They are bodies. The unseen ones include gods, spirits of the dead who never return to their bodies, spirits of the reincarnated who come back into new bodies, people who reportedly leave their bodies and come back to them immediately (see *Life After Life* by R.Moody), etc. Descartes took that two-fold classification and built his whole system of thought on it.

Pictures help to follow the history of 'the sciences' since then. Descartes drew a clear and distinct picture of a two-story universe. All bodies, including our own, are located on the lower story. We are souls, located on the upper story consisting of spirits. A central, most important feature of his picture is our body's **BRAIN**. Descartes was inspired to view the human body as a lifeless and soulless machine whose 'voluntary' [sic] movements are controlled by the **brain**. The **brain**, which is the control center of the body, is the only point of contact between us and the whole physical world. The body's senses, when stimulated by bodies outside our skin, send currents to the **brain** which correlate with the mind's sensory clues about what is happening out in the physical world. In response, we can (with God's help) indirectly influence the outer world by steering our body by steering currents flowing through the **brain**'s pineal gland. The two parts of Descartes' model became platforms for all modern 'scientific' research.

Physicists, chemists, and biologists began using the bottom half for various models of everything with shape and size. Descartes flirted with the idea that the physical world is really a huge ocean of matter in the form of infinitesimal granules which can do only two things: rest or move. If they move, it is because they are shoved, so he pictured the planets as being carried around the sun by a whirlpool of matter. Newton corrected that picture by thinking of the planets as moving in space that's so nearly empty that it offers little resistance to the free-floating planets. Biologists definitively confirmed our body's machine-like nature and turned biology into bio-chemistry and then bio-physics. The '**laws of physics**' are nothing but shorthand descriptions of what bodies (subatoms are the only ones that exist) can be expected to do in the future in light of what they've done in the past. Newton's 'laws,' for instance, only tell us where to look for bodies the next time we wish to check up on their whereabouts. P.S. To get some appreciation for the many-levelled difficulties involved in discovering such a vast repertoire of 'physical science' **laws** as the repertoire that can now be 'found' in the library, picture yourself watching while four invisible card-players sit down to play a large variety of card games. Imagine that only the cards are visible. It will be up to you to discover who or what the mover-players are, how they know what each other is thinking, whether the **rules** they follow are those for contract bridge, pinochle, gin, etc. Without ever having heard of cards, players, games, etc. Our ancestors, the first Adam and Eve, long ago plunked down in some jungle, savannah, plain, etc., were in a situation like that.

At the same time, the psychological science relating to things pictured in the upper half of Descartes' picture began to flourish as curious thinkers devoted more and more careful attention to the nitty-gritty details of our conscious experience. Locke started modern psychology by trying to prove, in enormous detail, Aristotle's thesis that every idea we have is built from tiny bits of information from the senses. In the course of his analyses, Locke suddenly realized that ideas of minds don't come from sensing bodies. His solution? The mind looks inward by 'reflection' at its acts, so its idea of itself is mostly concepts of mental processes. Berkeley took apart the ideas of outer 'bodies,' found they are just copies of inner sense-data, and so denied that we can know outer bodies as such. Using the same analytic method, Hume said "mind," "cause," and "God" name ideas related to other ideas, so he said we can't prove anything about minds, God, etc. Their pioneer attempt to look closely at each and every idea paved the way for Kant, Hegel, James, Freud, etc. QU: Did you get <u>a picture</u> of people dissecting ideas the way biologists dissect specimens?

If you meditate long and hard on the last question, you will be able to appreciate a major thesis of this quintalism: **we use images or pictures as aids in our thinking and**

reasoning. A good way to begin thinking about two major trends after Descartes is to picture some thinkers getting rid of Descartes' upper story and others getting rid of his lower story. In even simpler terms, some filled their inner, space-time model with bodies and nothing else (these got called "materialists"), some others felt the universe had all spirits and no bodies (these got called "idealists"). Advocates of the two-story view got called "dualists," the more radical simplifiers who claimed that only one story exists came to be called "monists." Still, monists do not begin with monism nor dualists with dualism. Materialists, idealists, and dualists are converts. All began their thinking careers by acquiring, between birth and birthday five or six, the *common*-sense theory. One part of that is good old naive-realism which tacitly includes quadruplism: bodies, living things, sentient things, and rational beings. That is why, even when we radically disagree as to which parts of **it** we agree with, we can still make-sense! of each other's non-sense! by referring back to it. Common-sense is our lingua franca. Is any of this making sense to you?

The quintalist, 5-item theory proposed here can be pictured as using a picture of a world that has five types of existing things in it: persons, their thoughts or theories, what they sense (colors, sounds, odors, etc.), faint copy-like images of what they've sensed, and—possibly— subatomsized bodies. The theory accompanying the picture holds that, if you are not a figment of my imagination, the thoughts you presently understand as you seem to run your eyes across and down these rows and rose of printed figures are your private thoughts. You can measure the truth of some of your most basic beliefs by

careful attention to reading: the thought this 'sentence' brings will remind you that this is not a sentence, that what you see are part of the colors 'making up' your total visual field, that—besides these sensed rows and rose and your thoughts—a constant haul of imagery is being dredged up from your ocean of sense-memories. (That image vivid enough?) Finally, if the world of subatoms described earlier isn't a figment of imagination, then out here in the utter darkness of vast, silent space, zillions upon zillions of inert, powerless protons, electrons, and photons are being put through their intricate choreography in synchrony with the constant streams of thoughts, imagery, and sense-data being created and offered to us billions of other human persons who, like you, are still in 'this' phase of our existence. God presides over everything according to this theory-model, just as God did according to the one Descartes, unless he is a figment of my imagination, held.

E. The origin of thoughts. The most influential thinkers in recent history have been the ones who offered a complete system, one that is not only about *what there is to know* but one that also attempts to explain *how we know what exists*. The task of finding the right combination of the two has led to shelf-fuls of ingenious theories. When Descartes arrived on the scene, the naive realism espoused by the medieval followers of Aristotle was still strong. They believed that, although sciences are the product of reasoning, the raw material for all the sciences comes from our sensing. Descartes challenged naive realism and found himself arguing that at least some of our ideas—those of God and the soul, for instance—must be from

God. Locke refused to accept any theory of inborn or innate ideas, and tried to find the origin of all our ideas in either sensory or reflective experience. The unsolveable difficulties Locke's Newtonian physics created taught Berkeley that, if the modern sciences are true, no one ever senses bodies and it's therefore impossible for anyone to prove that bodies exist or that s/he has any idea of what "unobserved and unobservable body" means. Hume used the same kind of reasoning to show that no one has any idea of what "unobserved and unobservable cause" means, so that traditional arguments about God are worthless. Kant tried to save some of tradition, but only by adopting the untraditional idea that the human mind is the source of the laws governing its 'world'! This radical suggestion opened the door to ever bolder and more radical theories about what exists and how we know. It eventually led to Einstein's idea that we can learn about nature with ideas freely created by our imagination.

We-create-to-discover is a temporary compromise. Kant's insight fits the fact that we all create the same original world-view. Given no choice, we learn it without knowing what we are doing. Einstein's insight fits the fact of later-on revisions of earlier base'ics. If you get that much, you are on your way to choosing which model of the world represents a discovery of the truth. That will 'create' your 'world.' But is it imposed on you by your senses? By your reading? One you've created? Or one offered by God? Incidentally, how did you learn all this history about Descartes, etc.?

F. Descartes' greatest blunder. Descartes did make errors. Big ones, in fact. For instance, he thought he had discovered a method, a set of rules, that would almost automatically lead to new discoveries. He argued at times that the soul and body make a single thing. But those were not his worst errors.

He blundered most of all by losing touch with experienced colors, sounds, tastes, heat, cold, and the other most obviously sensory existents of all. As a result, he eliminated them from his worldview. In place of colors, sounds, odors, tastes, etc., Descartes admitted only colorless, soundless, etc., ideas OF color, sound, etc. But, just as an idea OF Santa is not Santa, an idea OF color is not color or even colorED!

Descartes' blunder can be avoided by returning to the common-sense insight of Aristotle, an insight that was eventually re-discovered by Berkeley. For instance, even if we mis-identify the banana-shaped, disguised piece of wax and call it a banana, we can still be confident—as were all medieval thinkers who accepted Aristotle's theory about each sense having its 'special object'—that what we see has a yellow <u>color</u>, just as we can be confident that the tape-recording produces a <u>sound</u> almost exactly like her voice even though it's not her, that the carrot pie has the same <u>taste</u> as pumpkin pie does, etc.

Descartes was followed in his oversight by Spinoza, Leibniz, etc., but most distinctly and clearly by Newton: "...so colours in the object are nothing but a disposition to reflect this or that sort of rays more copiously than the rest; in the rays they are nothing but their disposition to propagate this or that motion into the sensorium, and in the sensorium they are sensations **of those motions!** [!?!!??] under the form of colours" (from his *Opticks*). The blunder is easily understood. So powerful is the grip of naive realism that even those who reject it in theory and who pay lip service to the formula that "color, sound, and other secondary qualities are in the mind" **rarely** make room for colors as such, sounds as such, or the smells as such which—every serious article on odor is compelled by tradition to mention them!—Marcel Proust wove into a well-known work. Who, when s/he remembers a piece of tea-dunked petite madeleine thinks of dancing atoms in an odorless brain? Gads! Unwittingly, we ignore what we experience and theorize about what we don't as if we do!

Why was it his greatest blunder? Not just because the things most certainly brought to our attention—except for pain and phantom limbs!—got ignored, but because the colors we experience are clearly and distinctly spread out in two-dimensions at least and seem like 3-D **proof for non-bodily extension**, a possibility for which there is no room in Descartes' improved but imperfect space-time model. Berkeley noticed the blunder. That's why he adds an essential corrective to Descartes' colorless palette. (See #6 and #7 in the following chapter.)

Do your thoughts about my thoughts about Berkeley's thoughts about Descartes' and Newton's thoughts about the colors (of?! what) *you* see! make sense? Do you know what aunt Nell thinks about Joe's feelings about Ida's opinions about her?

4. LOOSEN UP YOUR 'WORD' HABITS

1. At the mercy of words? Your task is to choose the true GUTE. Your chosen grand unifying theory, of EVERYthing!, will create your 'reality.' A child in the midst of a nightmare 'lives' amidst the world of that nightmare. After the child wakes and is comforted by mom, the child learns that the nightmare 'world' wasn't real. That means that, though it was real, it was only(!) real thoughts and real imagery. Your 'reality' seems to be that you are reading this book. As long as you keep reading it, you are at my mercy. The words on this page are the means whereby I control your thoughts as long as you are willing to sit there and keep reading. As soon as I finish these six re-meditations, I will be heading to Ohio to visit my family. You won't be involved in that at all. Use that fact to help you realize how dependent you are on words. You'll never know I went to Ohio unless you read this. Think how much you are at the mercy of all our words, all the words of us out here, "us" referring to your parents, teachers, newscasters, etc. So much at the mercy of our words are you that you'll have to take it on faith that I went to Ohio in June, '95, when you were totally preoccupied with other things.

So much at the mercy of words are you, that if I lie you may have no way of finding it out. Suppose you hire a detective to see whether I went to Ohio on June 4, 1995. (I did.) If I am lying (I am), how could you be sure I didn't pay the detective to lie, too? You'll be relying on words to correct other words. In fact, detectives make honest mistakes. That means you must trust that words are not conveying lies or, almost as bad, honest errors. Still, words appear indispensable. How much of what you've never personally witnessed—e.g., the billions of facts about China and the millions of Chinese living lives as richly-detailed as your own—could you know without the help of words? How much or little! would you know if you had been raised in the wild by wordless chimps? We are slaves to words, but they can mislead us.

2. Can words free you from slavery to words? No. Words do not exist. You were, in fact, raised in a wordless world by wordless humans. It is the myth—the erroneous thought that words exist—that you must free yourself from. If words exist and you learn from them, then you just learned from them that they do not exist. (By the way, you don't either.) If you believe that words and you exist—and both do—then you cannot believe what the preceding words 'told' you. If, that is, you can figure out which were referred to by "the preceding words." Did it refer to the ones before the sentence with that phrase in it or to the ones in the sentence that contained it? STOP. Does any of that make sense? In which sense? GO. To the library and read up on everything that comes under the umbrella phrase, "the Linguistic Turn." See how much help it gives you as you try to answer the two questions in? or behind? the double-meaning "Does any of that make sense?" Weigh that help against the advice of these (non) pages: "See for your self which total theory of everything offers the most adequate answers to these basic questions about word habits."

The real issue is not word habits, but thought habits. The thesis of the first three re-meditations is simple: each learner learns a commonsense theory whose 'vehicle' is inner, quasi-3D imagery of the outer world. Each learner in quest of certainty is well-advised to aim for an inner model that situates each existent, both space- and time-wise, vis-à-vis everything else, so far as that is possible. Today's learners who have access to well-stocked libraries will discover that they have a range of radically different models from which to choose an alternative to their early commonsense theory of everything. Among their options are the sophisticated naive realism of the Aristotelians, Descartes' sharp dualism, the materialists' and idealists' monisms, etc., each with endless minor variations. (There are, after all, billions of unique individual mindsets.) The only thing that will free you from slavery to the myth of language, if it still hobbles you (not your mind) in your quest for certain truth, is noticing that it is thoughts that are at the core of what you are doing now, and that you need the right thoughts about what you directly sense, meaning (once the shorthand "sense" is spelled out) thoughts about what you directly see, hear, smell, feel, etc., to help you decide what these rows and rose are that you see here. And here. And now here. Since we all grow up naively and mistakenly thinking we hear spoken words and see written ones, this means that freedom will come only when you get in the habit of applying the right alternative theory. Which is the reason why there's a full-page diagram at the end of this chapter. Look at it. What do you see there?

3. The stage is set by Commonsense Theory... which includes a-the fundamentals for all discussions about what is truth and what is error, b-fundamentals for facing the moral challenge to tell the truth, and c-naive realism. It provides the framework for making our moral choices vis-à-vis those neighbors mentioned in the "Love your neighbor as yourself" version of the Golden Rule. Most of us go through life never suspecting what an illusion its naive-realism one-third is, though, but when we do discover it and how prone we are to error from our earliest youth, we may wonder—like Descartes—how we got to be that way. Francis Bacon fingered the answer. We got this way because God chose to enrich our lives with the great game of wits called "science." D.Boorstin (if he lived), selected the following gem from Bacon (if he did) to serve as the epigraph for his 1983 history of science entitled *The Discoverers*:

> Nay, the same Solomon the king, although he excelled in the glory of treasure and magnificent buildings, of shipping and navigation, of service and attendance, of fame and renown, and the like, yet he maketh no claim to any of those glories, but only to the glory of the inquisition of truth; for so he saith expressly, "The glory of God is to conceal a thing, but the glory of the king is to find it out"; as if, according to the innocent play of children, the Divine Majesty took delight to

hide his works, to the end to have them found out; and as if kings could not obtain a greater honour than to be God's play-fellows in that game. (Francis Bacon, *The Advancement of Learning*, 1605)

Words—or what we are in the habit of regarding as words—are crucial to this game of wits. They provide the handles that allow us to gain control of our thoughts about the world. Our thoughts about the world use, as their 'vehicle,' the inner model which should be viewed as **a large-scale representation** with distinguishable sub-representations. Without 'word-handles' for the space-time model's parts, our stream of consciousness would be as limited to present sensings, memories of past sensings, and anticipations of future sensings, as the beasts' consciousness—if any exists—is limited to. But you just thought of far more. You just thought. Just?!

4. The Myth of Language. An old *commonsense* account of Helen Keller's discovery of the 'meaning' accompanying certain tactile sense-data helps to see 'language' for what it is: EXTRA sounds, ciphers, etc., plus ADDED memory-image associations.

Here was a small human being who at the age of 19 months had moved with appalling suddenness not only from light to darkness but to silence. My few words wilted, my mind was chained in darkness, and my growing body was governed largely by animal impulses... A sorrier situation never confronted a young woman with a noble purpose than that which faced Annie Sullivan. I recall her repeated attempts to spell words—words which meant nothing—into my small hand. But at last, on April 5, 1887, about a month after her arrival, she reached my consciousness with the word "water."

It happened at the well house, where I was holding a mug under the spout. Annie pumped water into it, and when the water gushed over onto my hand she kept spelling w-a-t-e-r into my other hand with her fingers. Suddenly I understood. Caught up in the first joy I had known since my illness, I reached out eagerly to Annie's ever-ready hand, begging for new words to identify whatever objects I touched. Spark after spark of meaning flew from hand to hand and, miraculously, affection was born. From the well house there walked two enraptured beings calling each other "Helen" and "Teacher."

Those first words that I understood were like the first warm beams that start the melting of winter snow, a patch here, another there. Next came adjectives, then verbs, and the melting was more rapid. Every object I touched was transformed. Earth, air, and water were quickened by Teacher's creative hand, and life tumbled upon me full of meaning... In a few days I was another child, pursuing new discoveries through the witchery of Teacher's finger-spelling.

Teacher wouldn't let the world about me be silent. I "heard" in my fingers the neigh of Prince, the saddle horse, the mooing of cows, the squeal of baby pigs. She brought me into sensory contact with everything that could be reached or felt—sunlight, the quivering of soap bubbles, the rustling of silk, the fury of a storm, the noises of insects, the creaking of a door, the voice of a loved one. To this day I cannot "command the uses of my soul" or stir my mind to action without the memory of Teacher's fingers upon my palm. (H. Keller, *Teacher*, chapter 5, abridged; *Readers Digest*, April, 1956.)

The lesson from Helen's dramatic words is that there was no natural-law, invariable link between her tactile sense-data and her thoughts. Helen already had constructed an inner, naive-realist model of her outer neighborhood. That is, she already had in place an enormously complex set of associated memory-images to serve as 'vehicle' for the thoughts 'making up' her commonsense belief-system. She already had one way to interpret the tactile sense-data—the hand-grabbings and palm-ticklings—she felt, and that was as nuisance behaviors by the newcomer trying to take over her life. *Then came the revelation that changed everything:* these were 'handles' to things already familiar to her. And 'handles' to the thoughts of someone with whom she could communicate once she acquired similar 'handles.' In other (non)words, this new realization (revelation, insight, hypothesis, inference...or just plain thought) gave her a whole new way to interpret the same sense-data. Which didn't change. Which were still just plain old hand-grabbings and palm-ticklings. Here, you are asked to go in a reverse direction. To take what you now mis-take for words distinct from sounds or ink marks and to reinterpret them as simply more different, varied, or dissimilar sounds and ink-mark colors. More of them. Extra ones.

Extra sense-data. Imagine yourself born into a trappist-silent world. The only sounds you'd hear would be the shuffling of feet toward your crib, rustle of blankets and diapers, singing of birds outside your window, crying from your own vocal chords, and so on. As it was, your infant world was filled with extra noises, with "What a darling!" and "Sshhh, mommy's here," sounds made by excited and solicitous adults. H.S.Sullivan's "A Theory of Interpersonal Relations" lecture of 1944 provides an ex-infant's description of the normal child's discovery of the power of 'words' as it relates to "mama." Children first form an inner model by associating certain memory-images of sense-data into complexes. Thus, the child, after many experiences of the 'mama' color-shapes, the 'mama' voice-sounds, the 'mama' felt-caregivings, associates those memories into a package which becomes a stable figure in the child's inner model of the 'world.' Over and over, the child also experiences extra *heard* sounds. Lots of them. At some point in time, the child utters one of them, the 'ma-ma' sound, in a situational context which the adults judge appropriate, and what a commotion ensues! Thus did we, as children, 'discover' the power of certain sounds.

Later on, we attached extra *visual* memories (of 'written words') to the extra sound memories (of 'spoken ones') attached to the mama-complex, daddy-complex, rattle-complex, etc., associations. We learned to link "yellow" to the sound linked to the color 'of' daffodils, to link "red" to the sound linked to the color 'of' the stop-light, etc. After thousands of hours of practice, you reached—if you are like me—a stage where the first person who'd tell you that meaningful sentences, e.g., this one, are not essentially different from meaningless scribbles, e.g., si ti elbissop ot tup sdrow no repap sdrawkcab*, would seem nuts. If you are like me, only long practice can replace your naive belief-habits about language with a recognition that they build on mistaken premises and thus add up to a gigantic set of easily-recognizable fictions—useful, even indispensable fictions—deserving to be called "The Myth of Language." It's an obvious myth, but one that stands in the way of most people's discovery of further scientific truths. (*Perfectly meaningful words spelled backwards?)

Especially of the truth that all so-called special methods—scientific, sociological, theo-logical—are fictitious. Few 'scientists' notice how naive they are about reading and about words. They rely on words as much as anyone else does. (Maybe even more?) Consider reports. One person can do only a tiny bit of research, even if that 'tiny bit' takes months, perhaps years out of one life. But each person needs far more results from far more research than s/he can do, with the result that each must take almost all her or his 'facts' from others' reports. Everything anyone believes on the word of dead people—and Copernicus, Kepler, Galileo, Newton, Roemer, Dalton, etc., are all dead—must be taken on faith in the tons of words they left behind. How naive of 'scientists' to ignore the questions, What are words? and How do they work?

Ockham's Razor is called for here. Whoever hears sounds and thinks they are also words is hearing double. Whoever sees shaped and arranged marks and thinks they are also words is seeing double. **Mystics must stop talking about things that cannot be put into words. NONE can, for there are no words.** And no meanings are carried piggyback on sounds or ciphers. A kiss is just a kiss. Dried ink blotches marking up nice clean sheets of paper are only ink blotches. Only their different shapes tempt you to distinguish them into "prose," "a Rorschalk Test," "a Necker Cube" (cube, my eye!), etc. Agree with him or not, Noam Chomsky has at least avoided the howler committed by those who believe there's more on paper than what can be seen with the world's most powerful microscopes. Had Ryle ever caught on, he might have called it, with his shrewd abusiveness, "The Ghosts-in-the-Ink-Marks Myth."

5. Options and choices. On the page after this chapter, you will find a diagram with "Interpret Me" at the top (henceforth the IMD, short for **I**nterpret-**M**e **D**iagram). What you decide you see there, you can apply to reading in general. After all, the identical mechanisms are used in writing *Brothers Karamazov*, *Kristin Lavransdatter*, and *Origin of Species*, and the identical mechanisms are used to read them.

So, what do you see when you look at the IMD? (Notice the power of imagination. If you made an all-out effort, could you pretend that the IMD is alive—the way Joe Campbell and so [or too] many imagine Earth/Gaia is!—asking you to interpret it?) What do you see? **You have choices.** There are the error-laden-perception answers of un-scientific people: "It's a page with 2 words at the top (or 1 imperative sentence, 4 syllables, 11 letters, or 4 vowels + 7 consonants); dozens of X's; a simple problem of arithmetic; etc." Naive sophisticates may say: "Many ink marks; shaped ink marks; many shaped and arranged ink marks; lots of dried black ink on white paper, etc." A chemist would be more specific about the ink, and a nuclear physicist who agreed with Ferris would get even more basic. Anaximander, reincarnated, might invoke Einstein's $E=mc^2$ formula, which appears to mean that energy and mass are inter-convertible but really means that energy and mass are appearances of one nameless substance. James would say it is only so much in the way of [private] sensations. The view here is that the IMD you will see will be *part* of a **TVF**, short for <u>T</u>otal <u>V</u>isual <u>F</u>ield of colors, in your mind. (N.B. "In your mind," here, means separate from physical bodies). Only *part* of the whole TVF: who sees just one small item at a time? Don't you see the things surrounding this 'page' just the way you'd see the surroundings of the tiny 'house' in a painting of a big 'valley'?

An aside. Some have said that the greatest of all the obstacles woven into this Game of Wits is the problem of **the one and the many.** William James wrestled with it for a lifetime. Without arriving at a final solution. There are actually *many* one-vs-many problems, even though they all come under *one* formula. That's one of the many. The IMD offers another: do you see one square or many Xs? Some thinkers will say "only many Xs," gestaltists would likely say "only one figure against the ground." (Indecisivists won't budge from "A square 'made up of' Xs.") The answer here begins "Things are what they are; our task is to acknowledge their existence, to classify them in relation to everything else (a basic principle: every thing is similar to everything else and different from it as well), and then to understand what, if anything, what-exists does and why." In this case, it is obvious that there are many X's, each adjoined by a white area and not by the black of any other X. There is no 'square' with four continuous, unbroken lines. When I open my eyes, though, a TVF whose colors are continuous with each other appears, and that TVF is utterly distinct from what, in english, I call "sounds," both are utterly unlike odors, those three are utterly dissimilar from pain, and as I think out this answer I am using my sense-data 'concept-cluster.' Warning. The more we narrow our gaze on a single issue such as "Do you see one thing or many?" in the IMD case, the longer and more complex our answers become. Such answers then often bog down in labyrinthine 'metaphysicizing,' because they're carried out within the context of the answerer's allegiance to a long-standing, wrong GUTE. End of warning. And of aside.

You have **choices of answers** to "What do you see when the IMD is directly present to you?" That choice of answers should fit with **all** the other choices you make on **all** the other basic options proposed to you. Especially about what you see, hear, feel, smell, etc. Call the sum total of what you sense "my field of experience." Call what you freely **choose** to make out of it "my 'reality'." The challenge is to **choose** the best GUT for EVERYthing. It must be simple. But it must be adequate, that is, not too simple. For instance...

6. A scientific materialist's GUTE. It's 1995. There is no longer any good excuse—unless it is honest ignorance—for still believing in naive realism. Let me begin to give you the true picture by quoting from "How Brain Waves Can Fly A Plane," by M.Browne, from page C1 of the *N.Y.Times* for Tuesday, March 7, 1995:

> **To be locked inside one's own head**—unable to speak, move a muscle or even an eyeball—is perhaps **the worst imprisonment** a person can endure. But new techniques in electroencephalography may soon make it possible for a totally disabled person

to communicate by directly controlling the faint electromagnetic signals emitted by his or her brain... For the first time, scientists at the New York State Department of Health in Albany recently showed that it is possible for a person using brain wave control alone to move a computer cursor around a display screen. (Emphasis added.)

That will give you the bare idea of Descartes' monumental discovery that the brain is the control center for the whole body. When you turn a page, it is only because your brain sends signals to unfelt arm muscles to move an unfelt hand to turn an unfelt page, and when your eyes scan the page, it is only because your brain is sending a constant flow of commands to your unfelt eye muscles. What do you feel and see? Out in the physical world, there is no heat or cold. It is only the flow of kinetic energy out of your skin that sends signals to your brain making it seem that something is cold or into your skin that...ditto...makes it seem something is hot. The roughness or smoothness of the paper, by triggering different signals to your brain, makes you think you feel a particular texture. The light reflected to your eyes sends signals into the back of your brain, etc., and the final network of brain waves will make you think you see a page out in front of you! It has taken centuries of often frustrating research to nail down the facts, but the article cited above will give you some idea of how greatly that research has succeeded. Now...

Now, try getting used to the rest of the truth. Your sensory 'field' creates one huge illusion. The best way to grasp the truth is to learn everything you can about **virtual reality**. The idea is simple. Your brain is like an electro-hallucinator. It creates the amazingly realistic illusion of a visual field, of quadraphonic sounds, and of all sorts of smells, tastes, and feels. Sensing can be compared to watching TV-programs. You turn on the TV. It's the 16th inning of an Indians-Yankees night game. A fan, you are soon absorbed by the game. But what are you experiencing? Only an off-hours scientist would say "A game." On duty, the answer would be "A TV telecast." Draw a Grand Space-Time Picture to grasp why. The game is going on in a stadium, far from your home and thousands of other homes in which you and others are—at the most—seeing similar TV-image**s** assumed to be representative of the stadium scene, and hearing sound**s** assumed to be like those reaching the broadcast booth. There is one set of players but thousands of picture**s** on thousands of TV screens, one set of vibrations but thousands of reproduction**s** from TV speakers. Thousands of fans in the stadium but hundreds of thousands of space-separated, couch-bound viewers with their thousands of individual eyes and ears getting light photon**s** and sound**s** travelling from TVs to couches and the thousands of **skull-encased brains** receiving nerve-impulse signals which their brains convert into 'virtual realit**ies**' which they will mis-take for the gam**e** itself in the stadium. Or at least for pictures and sounds on/in the TV. Until they discover that **their experience is limited to their brains.**

Extend the analysis to your reading. No reader will stop mis-taking what is really going on as s/he reads who does not think with precision, that is, in the terms of modern physics and physiology. Look around. Did you see any baseball stadium, any ball-players, TV cameras or microphones, living rooms, etc.? No. All you saw were the above black figures against the white 'background' which is not in back of the letters but surrounding them. And not even that. Out in the physical world, there is no color. Scientists discovered that fact centuries ago. Here is what Newton learned about color back in the 1600's:

> If at any time I speak of light and rays as coloured or endued with colour, I would be understood to speak not philosophically and properly, but grossly, and according to such conceptions as vulgar [naive] people in seeing all these experiments would be apt to frame. For the rays to speak properly are not coloured. In them there is nothing else than a certain power and disposition to stir up a sensation of this or that colour. For as sound in a bell or musical string or other sounding body, is nothing but a trembling motion, and in the air nothing but that motion propagated from the object, and in the sensorium 'tis nothing but a sense of that motion under the form of sound; so colours in the object are nothing but a disposition to reflect this or that sort of rays more copiously than the rest; in the rays they are nothing but their dispositions to propagate this or that motion into the sensorium, and in the sensorium they are sensations of those motions under the form of colours. (*Opticks*)

Generalize that for all 'sensing.' **You are not in touch with anything outside your brain or sensorium**, and the only things reaching that brain are the motions or nerve impulses that have had to travel along those transmission cables you call your optic nerve, auditory nerve, and so on. You are, in an old-fashioned picture popularized long ago, like a telegraph operator shut up in a back room (your brain). Outside signals come into the room, you send signals back out from the room, but you never leave the room. Einstein compared trying to learn what it is like in the outside world that we can't get at, to trying to learn what things are like inside a closed watch we cannot open. Completely shut off from the outside world, Einstein wrote, physicists cannot even imagine what it would be like to take a peek at it. But, just as you might be able to look at a watch's face, study how its hands move, and from such clues guess at what is behind the face making the hands move, you can study what gets to your brain and infer what the things outside it are like. You sense nerve impulses which you interpret **as** colors (the white 'paper' surrounding the 'black' figures), you hear impulses you interpret **as** sounds (from Perry Como's throat), you smell, taste, and feel (**as** odor, etc.) the other impulses coming through other transmission lines. It takes time to put all the signals together, which is why infants do not yet know what is really going on, and when they do, evolution has programmed them to create an inner world-model with its illusions of color, sound, warmth, freezing cold, etc. Only in modern times has the human race acquired enough science to help us realize how much of our everyday world is illusion, to realize that, in fact, only colorless, etc., material things exist. Which leads to the conclusion that "words" stands for things physical: air-vibrations, ink molecules, or brain waves—**as such!**—etc., depending on the context. Nothing else exists.

7. A quintalist's reply. The scientific materialist's model is immeasurably better than our naive-realist view. One provides a basis for destroying Hiroshima and Nagasaki immeasurably faster than the other. But three centuries ago, it struck the young Berkeley that the materialist picture was inadequate. **In a huge way.** In an absolutely, stunningly, blindingly clear way. Other great thinkers followed. Hume took his insight and became the first to track down its implications for the idea that we get ideas of cause-effect interactions from the senses: we don't. Kant then created a radical new theory to save the certainty of Euclid's geometry and Newton's physics from Hume's skeptical use of Berkeley's insight. So, what did Berkeley notice?

Materialists have no room in their Big Picture for the things Aristotle noticed we can be most certain of: colors, sounds, tastes, warmth, icy chills, pains, tickles, 'physical' pleasures, and—what everyone who studies French literature comes across—the odor 'of' a morsel of tea-soaked petite madeleine. Or any other scents, stenches, etc.

In a word, there are infinitely more things in heaven and earth—or would be if h & e existed—than there's room for in the materialists' philosophy. Materialists (and many non-materialists!) are theory-schizophrenics. In their naive-realist moments, which make up nearly all of their lives, they never hesitate to believe in colors, sounds, etc. They'd never go into a clothing store and ask for a shirt that has no color or reflects no light (black?). Never order a pair of pants that has all the colors or reflects all the light (white?). And never ask for some chemicals that will cause nerve impulses they can interpret as a coffee taste. But, if you ask them what they really! mean when they order a black shirt or white pants or cup of coffee, they instantly **call up on the screen of their imagination** the image of a brain receiving nerve impulses—today's "impulses" and Newton's "motions" are synonymous— and say that color as such and flavor as such do not exist, only impulses or motions interpreted **as** (today's formula) or sensed **under the form of** (Newton's) color or taste. But this is nonsense. Understandable nonsense. We do not sense motions. Or neutral neuronal impulses. We sense color and sound, which is why there is such a radical difference between the life-experience of someone born blind and that of someone else born deaf. As for a toothache-type of pain, who in their right mind seriously believes it is exactly the same thing as color and sound, i.e., just more homogenous motions or impulses, but interpreted this time '**as** pain'?!

The materialists' analysis of sensation stops one step short. Yes, common-sensically speaking, environmental objects send stimuli to our eyes, ears, nose, etc. Yes, the stimuli trigger nerve impulses that travel, via afferent nerves, to our brain. At that point, however, it is not simply our brain mis-interpreting colorless brain excitations 'as color,' noiseless brain excitations 'as sound,' etc. When the impulses reach our brain, immaterial colors, sounds, etc., are produced in our mind, and it is they that we experience.

Don't argue till you decide whether there is anyone to argue with. Straight-talking, consistent materialists agree with quintalism at least in this: you have never sensed another human. Like the TV viewer, you have experienced private TVFs and can only guess whether or not other people exist. **This is the heart of the Turing Test.** Take the materialist's baseball-game scenario the whole way. TV-viewing is like movie-going. When the movie-theater's lights dim and the blank screen seems to suddenly fill with color and the theater to fill with sound, what you really sense are private colors and sounds. **Your imagination supplies all the rest.** There really are no kissing Romeos, no treacherous Iagos, no hopeless Pollyannas, and so on. And what about the baseball game? When you can't sleep and turn on the TV at 1am, you may be viewing a late-night rebroadcast of an earlier game. You may assume that the stadium is lit up, that there are thousands of fans cheering their team on, when all the while the stadium is utterly empty and dark. Colors and sounds are supplied by the miracles of modern technology, and **your imagination supplies all the rest.** The question raised by Russell and Einstein— and by Descartes, Berkeley, Hume, Kant, and others before them—should be made more pointed. Not only how do we know that bodies exist? **But how do you know the stadium is not empty and dark?** How do you know you are not really alone, enjoying a 'virtual-reality' movie with no real bodies, no other 'minds,' and no thoughts on their in sides?

This is not a matter to be argued over. It is a matter for decision. The decision about whether you deal with inferred matter, immaterial phenomena, or both, relates to a total-system decision: **which GUTE accounts for all the evidence?** Materialists have no room for colors. Naive-realists and Berkeley do. And Hume, Kant, James, Mach, etc. To get a feel for how materialists think of rainbow colors, you can start with a convenient, up-to-date report on their thinking: C.J.Hardin's *Color for Philosophers* (1988). When you finish familiarizing yourself with the colorless, odorless, painless, and pleasureless 'world' of the materialists, you can immerse yourself in the works of Berkeley, Hume, and Kant, and thereby familiarize yourself with their views of a color-filled, odor-filled, pain- and pleasure-filled virtual-reality 'world' which these (non)pages! are a part of. Then check and decide: are these colors **as such**? Etc.

8. Adequate models and adequate semantics. This re-meditation—or chapter?—began with the words "Your task is to choose the true GUTE. Your chosen grand unifying theory, of EVERYthing!, will create your 'reality.'" What does "true GUTE" mean? What does "true" mean? For years, James fought with those who said "It means correspondence between thought and reality." Here's why.

We all begin with commonsense. None of us begins life with a clear and distinct idea that thoughts are things distinct from the things they are thoughts of. We first learn—it seems—about moms, dads, rattles. About realities, period! (Given ex-infants' complete amnesia and pre-ex-infants' agreement to not give interviews, such claims about infants are, as C.D.Broad noted, precarious.) So long as the rattle is within sight, it exists, but out-of-sight at first means out-of-mind. But after we learn that we can have nightmares of events that are not happening and thoughts of what no longer or not yet exists, we build those facts into our model by imagining that we have things inside us—hence the early importance of our skin for getting clear and distinct about these matters—which are distinct from outside ones. If we grow up among 'enlisters,' we begin to use "ideas" and "thoughts" for those things which must be included with heart, stomach, teeth, and other inside items. Then we learn about representations: some drawings are life-like, some are not. How natural to apply this to thoughts and to say that a true thought is one that matches reality. Till we learn that we can't sense the realities out there, which means we can't compare our thoughts with them. Till we confront the fact that, even if there are bodies out there, a thought can't literally be like a body or like anything but an identical thought. Etc.

Our first response to such shocks is to keep our original commonsense thought-habits as much intact as possible. We begin what can only be described as a long series of attempts to eat our cake and still have it. Especially in how we talk. We change our theory but keep old word-formulas by re-defining the terms. Berkeley grew up believing in apples, oranges, a mouth to eat them with, the sun, etc. On the outside of his skin, brain, and mind. He later changed his mind. But, he refused to say that such things do not exist. He redefined "apple," "orange," etc., the same way that a columnist insisting that there is a Santa has to redefine "Santa." Did Berkeley, Kant, and James believe in apples? It all depends on how you define...

Define everything. Including "define." The cure is making talk fit clear thought. Defining involves a partial tour of one's mindset. The most common question used by sincere inquirers and debaters is "What do you mean by ___?" Answering in a language the inquirer does not understand is of no help to the sincere. Giving either the materialist's colorless or Berkeleyan-phenomenalist's bodyless answer to "What do you mean by 'a red apple'?" is answering in a language other than that used for our everyday, commonsense GUTE. Materialists can debate fruitfully about the mind with those who agree to use "mind" to think about the brain or its functions. Berkeley'an phenomenalists (re bodies) can debate fruitfully about brains with those who agree to use "brain" for orderly sequences of sense-data the way movie-goers should use "Snow White." ("Snow White won't die" means there will be more 'Snow-White' colors and sounds.) The issue is not what we call things, but what we believe there is to call. That is the only adequate solution to the semantic issues so heatedly debated in this era by phenomenologists, neo-positivists, ordinary language analysts, et al.

9. Adequate thoughts. Consider semantic debates as simple math problems. How do you count? How many things? How many classes of things? Be exact in your count, but flexible in how you cue. Most people in the world do not use english cues anyway. Any cues whatever will serve the purpose (notice the switches from roman to arabic to binary in the re-meditations' titles?), so long as everyone understands everyone else's—and her/his own!—meanings well enough.

Do you see ink marks, moving atoms, neural quiverings, etc., that you mis-took for words? Or does the universe include **more!** than physical things? At the very least these things that you see? And these? And these? Your style of answering this will reflect your style of confronting all hard decisions. Relate the question about what you see to the question about God. Does nature act alone? Has a big glob of matter self-organized its self into this universe whose operations display a level of law-fulness dazzling to behold? Meditate on how the gooey stuff inside an egg self-organizes into the dazzling little self-propelling chick that breaks out of the shell. The atheist claim is that the universe as a whole is like that. Or does 'your mind' tell you "**There just has to be more!**"? How many things are there? How do you count? How do you classify? Are "brain" and "mind" two names for one thing? For two things? For more? What kind/class? What about "motion in the brain" and "color"? Etc.

As you scan these rows and rose, do thoughts come to you? Do you understand them? Even if you do not agree with them? Where, then, do thoughts fit in?

INTERPRET ME

ONE (SQUARE) THING? OR MANY (X-SHAPED) THINGS?

REALIST NOMINALISM OR NOMINALIST REALISM

We think and use images at the same time. Our grandest (non-bodily) image is of the infinite-space cosmos which contains zillions upon zillions of subatom-sized bodies, each as real as the rest, and each doing nothing but stand still or move. That image of bodies provides a setting that enables us to think about non-bodies. As long as we can focus on them selectively.

How, when it is necessary, can we think (and talk) selectively about just some of those bodies and not the rest? By inventing special concepts. The idea is simple. Suppose we could stop all the subatoms in their tracks. That would allow us to take an inventory of their number, their exact locations, even their shapes and sizes. (No masses or charges, though.) It would also allow us to notice that some of them congregate as if to form groups. Today's astronomers begin with the galaxy-concept. "Galaxy" is useful for speaking simultaneously about zillions of subatoms more tightly clustered than, say, clouds of less-close hydrogen atoms floating in the areas between galaxies. Armed with such a concept, we imagine galaxy-clusters strung out in space somewhat like the separate storm-spirals strung out across the Atlantic from Africa to the Carribean which, during the autumn hurricane season, we six-o'clock-weather-report viewers see in satellite photos. Then we give them proper names the way we give the storms proper names. Our galaxy is named the "Milky Way." "Star" and "planet" cue smaller-group concepts used to mentally focus on (relatively!) fewer of the zillion-times-zillions of subatoms.

To zoom in even closer to the bodies to which *each non-body-person's stream of consciousness* is directly 'related,' we have other, smaller-group concepts. We zoom in to the planet-sized cluster named "Earth," then make use of the concept named "continent" and any others used for areas that people agree to mentally mark off and name. With such concepts, you can mentally locate the subatoms you call "my body" and then "my body's brain." Still-smaller-group concepts are named "neuron," "dendrite," "atom," etc.

With the universe thus stopped for inventory, we can use other arsenals of concepts. "The text of Romeo and Juliet" is shorthand, useful for referring to all the subatoms which, we say, 'make up' the individual 'copies' of either the original which Shakespeare wrote or of a translation of it into Russian, French, etc. "Book" is a useful way of making shorthand reference to each cluster of those subatoms, and sub-clusters can be mentally 'pointed to' by the concepts cued by "bound pages," "a sheet of paper covered with ink marks," "a sentence," "the letter a," "the letter t," "the letter o," "the letter m," or—more globally—by "a word" (e.g., "atom") or—more generically—by "one ink mark." Etc.

This should give you some clues to how one person views things. And why he regards "**THE** text of Romeo and Juliet" (if taken as a singular name for a singular real thing) to be the (non)name for a non-existent. And why, if you transfer this pattern of analysis to non-bodily, immaterial realities, you will find that the number of non-existent fictions is in the thousands. Or millions.

0101. EVERY PLEASURE COMES WARM FROM THE HAND OF GOD

a. Cogito, ergo sum. There are many things to be grateful to Descartes for. He used his knowledge of physics (light, lenses, etc.) and physiology (the role of the eye's lens vis-à-vis light, etc.) to lay the groundwork for psycho-physics or—more specifically—psycho-neurology which focusses on the role of the *brain* in relation to conscious experience. He brought Plato's flight into the clouds of abstraction back to the earth of *single existents* by stressing—Ockham-like—the fact that the only thoughts any real thinker understands directly belong to the one thinker whose pleasures that thinker can both understand thoughts about and simultaneously feel. And, even if he failed to do as much justice to sense experience as Berkeley, Hume, and Kant did later, Descartes did what Berkeley and Hume utterly failed to do: recognize the distinct-from-sensing-and-imaging *role of thought*, and thereby set the stage for such giant thinkers about thought as Kant, the Fichte-Schelling-Hegel trio, the duo of Husserl and Heidegger, and—in between them—the greatest of all, James. It was Descartes, though, who started the ball rolling for modern thinking about thought, a claim proven by the fact that in 1995 AD "Cogito"—latin for "I think"!—is universally recognized as the one-word sentence which sums up Descartes' entire philosophy. (What? Some of the earth's 5.7 billion inhabitants don't recognize the *Cogito*?!)

Did some thoughts just come to you? Why aren't you answering? Is it because, like one bahaviorist professor teaching behaviorism to his class, you are waiting for someone to show you a thought? Or because, like Socrates who bumped into Meno that fateful afternoon so long ago on an Athens street, you want to be given a definition first? See whether or not you can understand *what I tell you next*. No one can show you a thought. You cannot look at one. The only thing you can do is understand a thought when one comes to you. Nor can it be defined. There is no word "thought," so there's no it to be defined. In fact, there are no definitions, neither the verbal kind made of words (which do not exist) nor the pointing type (there are no fingers or arms to point and, even if there were, you'd never see one). Did any thoughts just come to you? Did you understand them? If you didn't, then see if scanning the next little black figures evokes any. If no thoughts are coming to you, stop reading. Either you aren't old enough. Or not brite enuf. Or u r old and brite enuf, but have an LD, short for Learning Disability. That means you need either a pill or improved habits or both. (Would Ryle approve?)

b. The goal is science. Of course, there is science and then there is science. Some of the ancients recognized what the wisest always recognize, namely, that old folk who have had no formal education often have a wisdom that only the young who are wise beyond their years possess. That insight is a commonplace in the handed-on wisdom called "perennial." When, that is, it's not called "good commonsense" or "good horse sense." (When the calling is done in english, of course.) Why mention that fact? Descartes and his successors would answer that "philosophy" was called "wisdom" by Aristotle, and during the middle ages, both philosophy and theology were known as wisdom—human and sacred, respectively—and defined as science.

Is there any best way to divide or carve science up? M.Gardner, who shocked some of us with his wise *Whys*, sorted science into good, bad, and bogus. Which, to any who have not 'loosened up' on the semantics, would seem to involve him in one of the things all pursuers of good science must be-wary of, a contradiction in terms. M.L.King once cited Aquinas' claim that a bad law is no law at all, which makes it difficult to understand something we all understand with perfect ease, namely, the distinction between good laws and bad ones. (Of course, there are no laws at all, not even one, so there can't be any ones in the plural, either.) But saying "Bad science is science" may be a bad thing for a scientifically-minded person to do, for too much bad saying leads to bad thinking, as Socrates noted just a few minutes before he died. Then again, if you spend enough time in the library, you will discover how many different fictions different writers use the english "science" as a cue for. Either when they call science a "sacred cow," call creationism "science," insist that that's abusing it, or warn that at least it or that has put it on trial. (A note on identifying referents. Identifying them is not only indispensable, it is relatively easy once we are familiar with the references, allusions, clues, etc., to them. Early in life we are equipped with the necessary skill, as is clear from the fact that even little kids can handle instant switches in reference involving "I" and "you." And mystics are in no doubt about who is reporting and who is listening as they describe the raptures in which their identity dissolved.) Did thoughts just come to you? Could you tell when they were clear vs when the references or allusions made the clues a bit difficult to figure out? I.e., could you tell the difference between vague or ambiguous ideas (better called "thoughts"), as opposed to those Descartes and scientists aim at, namely, clear and distinct ideas, that is, thoughts with clarity and precision? Then, despite it all, you should eventually be able to get the general drift of "Science: good, bad, and bogus."

Which is good, because libraries offer all different varieties. By picking out the good from the rest, we can fill information gaps and learn connections and distinctions that help us convert fuzzy thoughts into clearer ones. Consulting books that help us learn what great thinkers thought about thought is indispensable for converting our fuzzy thoughts about thinking into more distinct ones. There are books that tell us who those great thinkers are. There is a major problem, though. The book-guides do what the great thinkers do: contradict each other. Some will direct you to Plato, Aristotle, etc., while others will tell you that most of what Plato, etc., wrote is non-sensical because it is neither tautological nor sense-verifiable. Some will send you to writers who think, as Descartes did, that thought is a conscious phenomenon; but others will assure you that belief in such allegedly private stuff as consciousness is unscientific and send you to behavioral or neurobiological psychologists. Libraries—if they and books existed—offer clashes of opinion on every imaginable topic. That means that you must make up your own mind who is telling the truth. Not 'telling the truth' as when the teller is not deliberately trying to lie or deceive, but 'telling the truth' in the sense that what is told is true. Remember that someone who is honest may deceive you. Someone who lies may unintentionally say what is true. (I'm lying; the last two sentences are false.) And you cannot be sure someone is telling the truth unless you have reason to be sure s/he exists, is saying something, you understand what s/he is saying, s/he knows what s/he is talking about, etc. Are your standards for taking humans' words lower than Locke's standards for taking God's? THINK: Do you think I am telling you the truth?

c. Mapping out a thought's unity. If, when you finish reading *Re-Meditations*, you step back and think about the argument as a whole, you can think about it from several points of view. One way is particularly important: the book as a whole is about thoughts. *Re-Meditations* attempts to weave everything together this way: everything that exists and that you can learn about is something you can understand truths about **only through thoughts**. That is because only thoughts are either true or false. Revert to your naive realism. The sun has existed for eons, but the sun is not true. It may be large, it may be hot, and it may be far away, but it is not true. Photos of the sun exist, but they are not false. They are small, cool, and very close, but they are not false. "Sun" is a word, but you would be puzzled if—out of the blue—I came up and asked, "The sun: true or false?" But if I asked, "Can you name one thing that is very large, very hot, and very far away?", I would be quite surprised if you would not admit that "The sun!"—a complete sentence—is true. (Unless you didn't speak english.) The same way every complete sentence in this paragraph is true. Unless every one is false or unless some are true and some false. Or would be if sentences existed. They don't. **But sensible or empirical things—"sentence," "paragraph," etc.— are needed to think precisely about (fictitious) parts of unsensed thoughts.**

"Sentence," etc., are parts of the "language" arsenal of 'fictions.' It is one of dozens of arsenals of 'useful fictions.' For instance, to talk of only some (not all) of the 5.7B earthlings, we use our arsenals of place concepts. Of continents: Africans, Asians, etc. Of continental subdivisions made with lines invisible from helicopters: Alaskans, Canadians, etc. From there we go to New Jerseyites, New Yorkers, etc., to upstate apple-knockers, city-dwellers, etc., to uptown rich, slum poor, etc. In the end, there are still only 5.7B humans, because the grouping is all mental. (Cross-grouping is equally easy: Catholics vs Protestants around the globe, republicans vs democrats in the US, etc.) Here, with the arsenal of 'theoretical construct(ion)s' that come under "language," I can make precision references: to the entire work titled *Re-Meditations*, to Remed 0101, to section-a (Cogito...), to the last paragraph, the previous sentence, **this precise phrase**, its middle word's two syllables, its i, that i's dot, etc. But all these varied arrays of conceptual 'tools' require a thinker with an entire mindset-context to use them in referring to...? What **is** there to refer to?!

Did any thoughts just come to you as your eyes scanned those rose and roes? (From what I am told, such misspellings often irritate. I have reduced their number but will risk the side-effect consequence, both as a reminder that seen ciphers 'trigger' memory-images of previously-heard sounds and, even more, to provide evidents that human planners can freely adjust means to reach such goals as providing more evidents that humans are not machines, unless "machine" is made synonymous with "person.") If so, they were your thoughts, easiest thought of as things inside you. No definition now. Only description. Which begins with your everyday, up-to-date view of the universe. Zoom in to the Milky Way, our local star, our planet, the continent, nation, state, city, street, street number, floor, room, and area of the room your body presently occupies. If you enroll in certain types of mind-control courses, you will learn to become aware of tension which—in *seeming*! contrast to these rose and roes—is inside you and which, given the hectic pace of modern life, you barely notice. You will discover that you feel tension in different parts of your body and learn how to get rid of it through relaxation practices. (Agree or not, did you understand that?) You can also begin studying inner memory-images, thought by most to be faded sensations stored away till they are retrieved and studied, tho in fact they are brand new creations *ex nihilo* (from nothing) the same way that every TVF we see after a blink is brand new, the same way that the colors which appear when we put gentle pressure on our closed* eyelids are created, brand new, on the spot, no matter how 'exactly similar' the new are to the old. (Whether you agree or not, contradictory thoughts about memory-images just came to you, no?) Now for point one of this train of thoughts: **memory-images of sense-data (re)appear where the original data were sensed.** Take pain. "Pain" there is shorthand for individual pains, and even if you are not now feeling any, you will—if you are like me—notice that your attention is directed toward different parts of your 'body' when you (re)call them. Recall what a toothache on the right side of your mouth would feel like, then what banging your left knee on the sidewalk felt like (the ache takes a moment to 'develop' but then...!), next turn your attention to where you would expect to feel a stomach ache. All different places, right? And where do you remember the colors showing up when you gently press your closed eyes? Point two: if thoughts about 'pain in general,' about pains in various places, and about TVFs came to you, *where were the thoughts?* Third, (re)view this paragraph and see whether the following fits: you were invited to use your inner map to help you understand the claim that three types of things can exist inside you, namely, **sense-data** (pains, etc.), **images** (of pain, etc.), and especially **thoughts** (of sense-data, images, and thoughts). (*Do you close your eyes or do the lights go out? Eye-muscle-tensing data, etc., serve as clues.)

Next, recall Zeno's idea that there's never more than one time at a time. Can you ever think more than a single whole thought at a time? When you compare two contradictory claims, don't you have to do it with one thought? By remembering the first claim while thinking about the second or the second while thinking about the first and comparing both to the evidents? Think about that. Then ask yourself: what is the difference between *thinking about* the last severe pain you felt and what caused it and *remembering* that last pain and its cause? While doing so, be sure not to forget that, in both cases, your thoughts are distinct from the memory-images that accompany them. And be sure to remember that, whether or not you agree, the claim that images do accompany every thought is a claim being made through all six remediations. By the way, did you think I meant two different things in the last two sentences by "be sure not to forget" and "be sure to remember"? Or don't you remember? What do you think now when you do remember and compare the two? Or can't you keep track of so many things at once? James said he thought about this problem of how we know many things at once, over and over, for years. It is one of the biggest one-vs-many problems. Can you understand *and hang on to* all of this?

d. The Rorty Test. Why so much "Do (can) you understand?" Mostly to counter the after-effects of the Linguistic Turn and Behaviorist Psychology. But also to counter some 'science' myths they built on and the 'revelation' misconceptions which spark so much 'religious' strife. Truths cued by the good 'science' contents of the library are needed to sift the valuable truth from the damaging errors in those views. But library contents, like these, are useless unless understood. Do you understand?

God's Game of Wits is no easy 5-piece puzzle. It has 1,001 genuine pieces plus 50,001 false-lead ones thrown in to throw us off. Solving the mystery-of-the-mind area requires hours upon hours in the library in order to get a handle on the 'science of mind' begun before Parmenides, almost brought to a halt by his logical attack on logic showing that plurality and change are irrational, brilliantly restored by Plato, sharpened by medieval debates about universals, fused with brain studies by Descartes, pursued into the thinnest stratosphere of abstraction by Kant, idealists, and phenomenologists, but—once again—nearly brought to a screeching halt by the Linguistic Turn to endless explorations into our predictably un-rule'y 'language' use and the Behavioral Turn to verbal behaviors. The Linguistic Turn has run its course, the Radical Behaviorism that ran alongside it is dying a slow death. It is time to re-enter the library and do what we are supposed to do there: pick out all the essential pieces of truth and see what emerges once they are all put together in the right way. Does this picture have a ring of plausibility to it? Can you get the drift of the last sentence, even though it switches pictures? Or mixes metaphors. Or...

If you can (get the drift), then you have passed what I am taking the liberty of calling "The Rorty Test" in honor of the writer who, on page 88 of his *Philosophy and the Mirror of Nature* coming-to-grips with the same history of thought about thought, wrote that "Everybody understands everybody else's meanings very well indeed." True, none of us knows what anyone means at the very moment we emerge from the womb, and students prove on their exams that they did not always understand their prof's meanings, everyday facts that R.Rorty tacitly assumed his readers would understand, especially given the fact that he did not mean everybody, i.e., was not thinking of everybody, when he wrote his non-words. With enuf time, effort, IQ-power, and grace, thuf, everybody eventually can learn what any particular other person means. Agree or not, you do understand?

e. Every theory about thoughts 'rests on' imagery. At first, we are intimidated by the unfamiliar, abstract jargon used in college texts. Till we notice that it feeds off our everyday commonsense world-model. Proof? If you are like me, you could follow Helen Keller's story about how Annie taught her a new language, and you could do it with no prior courses in logic, hermeneutics, linguistics, or psychology. But you couldn't take any courses in anything without the language-learning needed to follow her story. (Agree or not, you at least understand, no?) Now watch.

(I believe) Aquinas was right to adopt Aristotle's claim that imagery accompanies all thinking. So, we need the right picture for thinking. That we understand thoughts is a fact. I clipped an article "Here's a Big Surprise: Homework Is Disliked" from the 2-21-89 *N.Y.Times* to prove it. It says "The students were asked to write down their thoughts when signaled every two hours or so." I have another one on the desk in front of me which says that every religion offers instructions for meditating and that one rule is to avoid getting distracted by irrelevant thoughts. Find a man or woman who can't understand that, and you'll have found someone who never meditated or is illiterate, severely retarded, senile or... (If such claims upset you, regard it as evidents that you passed the Rorty Test. If such misspellings do...)

(I'm sure) Plato constructed a model that helps us begin putting order into our thoughts about thinking. Which is only one of the many things we do. We walk, we talk, hear, see, etc. We walk with our legs, talk with our vocal chords, hear with our ears, and... But what do we think with? We do the thinking, Socrates (Plato's mentor) proposed that we are souls, so souls do the thinking. In his *Republic*, Plato built the framework for Aristotle and subsequent thinkers by picturing the soul as having organs, powers, or parts, much as the body has sense-organs. We souls have a reasoning part (intellect or mind) to think with, a desiring part to be moved by, and a spirited part (will) to take charge with. His theory about us souls using our intellect to know ideas parallels the image of us using eyes to see likenesses (images). All theories about knowing and thinking are built on pictures.

(I am convinced) Newton plus Descartes plus Berkeley add up to a very adequate picture to use in guiding our efforts to notice the reality of thoughts. Newton's idea of an all-inclusive space and duration offers the matrix image that helps us locate our own body vis-à-vis every other body. Thinking about what is inside our body's skin helps us notice our inner spread-out, ever-changing *sense-data* (and spread-out *imagery*!) which are distinct from outer *3D bodies*. To 'rise above' sensing and imaging, we must try to notice a fourth **MORE!** beyond ('meta,' 'trans,' over and above, in addition to) the first three. That is, to notice complete *thoughts*.

(I think) Plato, Aristotle, Aquinas, Descartes, etc., were wrong. (Take the Rorty Test on that.) Not wrong about everything or even most things. Here, I am zeroing in on their idea that the fourth MORE! has parts, *especially that it is made up of really distinct ideas or concepts.* Their thesis seems plausible enough. In the world there are plurals of most things: plural people, many animals, numerous plants, countless stars and grains of sand. So, there must be distinct ideas for those distinct things: the idea of person for people, of animal for beasts, of plant for vegetables, etc. Finally, as a quick glance at the preceding rose and roes will show, there are distinct *words* to go with distinct *ideas* of distinct *things*. That is the skeleton on which **Aristotle** hung his 'logic': we use *language symbols* for *mental concepts* of *real things*. He set the agenda for centuries of thinking about thought. The fourth MORE!, thought, was approached as if made up of parts. Thought is 'made up of' propositions 'made up of' single concepts. Did thoughts, however vague and nebulous on details, come to you just now? If so, then you are ready for a counter-proposition that has no parts.

(Cogito) Succeeding at God's Game of Wits has required learning how God 'directs ' the symphony of creation. How the stop-and-going of each subatom is correlated with the stop-and-going of every other subatom. How the creation of each person's sense-data is choreographed with an eye on that person's 'brain-subatoms,' an eye on the same person's other sense-data, and a third eye on the same person's images. How the creation of each person's imagery is choreographed with one eye on that individual's 'brain-subatoms,' one eye on the same person's sense-data, one on the same person's other images, and another on the same person's thoughts. Etc. (Note again: **'Word' sense-data link up directly with imagery, not thoughts.**) But thoughts have no parts, and there is no dividing line between one thought and the next. P.S. James' extensive writings are among the best sources of all for meditating on this 'unity' issue. Every GUTE has profound mystery lurking beneath surface clarity, and this-quintalism's debts-owed-for-surface-clarity are consolidated under the cue, "thoughts." The key to not getting lost is Rorty's Commonsense Test.

f. A favorite image. There you are, awake and alert. Conjure the following picture. There is a current of 'experience' flowing by in front of you. The sense-data directly related to your now-thoughts are these tiny black figures passing through the fovea'l area of your TVF. As they pass, they fish up a stream of tangled images which you can pretend are from an enormous store of past-experience memories. OK, are you ready? Do you have those items fixed in place? See now if you can notice that there is MORE!: **a cloud of meaning** hovering just above the fast-flowing imagery. It is a thousand-faceted, kaleidescopically-flashing, constantly-changing **cloud of meaning**. QU: Meaning of what, though? AN: The meaning of **all** the words. Repeat:

A THOUGHT IS THE MEANING OF ALL THE WORDS.

All the words in the sentence especially, but also all the words in its paragraph, on its page, of its chapter... Applied: these are word-clues to a portion of my GUTE, the earlier 'words' being clues to my mindset-context, these current 'words' cues for the focus. That is imagery, however. Fringe and focus merge indistinguishably into one another. Or would, if they were two distinct things. It is clear that you can think selectively of some things and not about others. These words are your clues to what in particular I was thinking about at 8:26:19 pm today, earlier words were clues to parts of my mindset-context. Here! (So great a mystery, such tenuous clues.)

g. Defense. Those who think that *mastery of logic* will help them discover the truth are utterly mistaken. Whitehead, co-author of the monumental 1910 work on logic which got around to 1+1=2 on page 362, was right to say later that "Logic, conceived as an adequate analysis of the advance of thought, is a fake" (1941). One reason is quite logical: logic is a fiction and doesn't exist. Another reason comes from history. Whitehead's collaborator was Russell, and their subsequent *disagreements* prove decisively that their logic didn't protect one or both from later mistakes. Thirdly, the 'language' of logic is like mathematical notation: it is an extra set of ciphers that have no meaning whatever in themselves. The formal proof is contained in an extremely condensed formula: $E^2=P(fa \cdot m^{100})xQ$. In all fairness, it must be added that Whitehead added this: "It [logic] is a superb instrument, but it requires a background of common sense." That applies to math, too. Or would...

Tho thoughts have no parts, sense-data are distinct: colors from sounds, black from white, one black figure from another, etc. The correlations between quasi-part-ful sense-data and images and partless thoughts are a necessary **plus**, but they seduce entrants in God's Game of Wits into a **minus**, namely, into adopting the proposal that thoughts, too, have parts. But God provides hints to help you cut through the deceptions. To do so, you must keep track of all the preceding...words?! (A major hint.) At least all that precedes which is crucial for understanding what comes next: **Cogito.** Count to see how many parts that thought has. Two? The action (thinking) plus the actor (a thinker)? Don't you wish! Zoom in to c what u think of when u c "thinker." One organism, one soul, or one body-plus-soul? The last? Re-count: I, a body-plus-soul, think. Be careful. Do "I" and "body-plus-soul" stand for one idea, two thoughts, or for three? Do you perhaps do what Descartes did most of the time, and regard the soul alone as the person? If so, go back and re-view the thought that came to you earlier when your eyes scanned ciphers like the following: "We walk, talk, hear..." Are you ready to put two and two together and conclude that none of us ever walks, talks, etc.? After all, you must see that, if it is not we who run over the cat but our car which does, it is not we who walk but our body, right? Are you ready to decide whether your body acts on its own as Huxley insisted, or acts in a way that you influence in some way at least, as James retorted? Do you subscribe to the most up-to-date physics? If you answered "Yes," then have you put four and two-more together yet and realized that no bodies of the size and make that Descartes, Huxley, or James usually had in mind even exist? In other cues, has it struck you that there is no walking, talking, etc., anywhere in the known universe? **A TEST: If a complete thought just came to you, count its parts.** P.S. Ask why logicians mostly ignore the fact that reasoning can be carried on for great lengths with no declarative sentences. (Imperative) Don't they know how Socrates instructed Meno's slave? (Interrogative) Look above and re-view what is between **Cogito** and here. Notice?

[Descartes deserves enormous credit for his treatment of the body and of the actual experience we naively mis-*think* is of our body. Like James, he recognized the unity of consciousness, which is precisely why he settled on the pineal gland as the point in the brain where physics and psychics interactively meet. He stressed the fact that amputees have experiences—vivid ones!—which are indistinguishable from those of non-amputees. He integrated phantom-limb experience into brain science, and later research has abundantly supported his conclusion: regardless of the body's behavior, *we* **experience** *nothing unless and until a stimulus reaches the brain*. He did make mistakes; he was a pioneer. But many who excoriate him show either a lack of information or of insight. To introduce the puzzles faced by Descartes and all who try to explain 'somatic' experience, O.Sacks' *A Leg to Stand On* is perfect. **End**.]

Part of solving one-and-many problems is boldly declaring that only wholes exist. Like Romeo and Juliet, parts are fictions: they don't exist, period. But thoughts do. Whoever can understand the thought <u>that</u> Romeo does not and never did exist, can also understand <u>that</u> parts do not exist. Even if s/he disagrees. Or course, nothing is easier to do than thinking that partless wholes have parts, which is why we all do it. Assume that light-photons are the smallest bodies that exist. Next, picture yourself enlarging one. What seems more natural than saying it has both a top and a bottom half, a right and a left half, surface and inside, etc.? Till it is cut, though, no halves. Even after it is cut, no halves. After you cut a whole stick in half, you will have two whole sticks, each half as long as the now defunct old whole: two wholes, no parts. The puzzle about taking a boat, replacing one old board with a new one each year until all the originals are replaced, then asking "Is it the same boat?", is a pseudo-puzzle: all that existed at the start were many whole boards, no boat. Aquinas used the mental-distinction solution for God, essences, etc. It applies equally to thoughts.

h. Evidents. "Iron curtain" is the picture for pessimists, "ravishing show" the one for optimists. Pessimists are those who say "Sense-data cut me off from all direct access to the world." Optimists now are those who discover that 'nature' is a private show but find no reason not to take the same attitude that naive-realists have when they (seem to) look at nature and marvel at the deity 'behind' it. There is no proof that our real situation is not, so far as persons go, just as we thought it was while we were growing up. True, once you 'see through' the Creators' trick, you discover that the tasty red apple hanging amid the green leaves is, if anything, zillions of tasteless, colorless, etc., subatoms dancing in the dark, but the taste, the color, the feel—all the things you prized in the first place—change not one whit. Even the pleasures which some think are 'lower' than the belly remain the same and, it seems, in the same place. The big shock in all of this is not that *unsensed* bodies lose their importance. (Huxley should have seen—as Berkeley did—that bodies, not experience, are the side-show). For anyone not used to meditating on how lonely one can be in a crowd, the sense of being cut off from all direct access to other people is the real shock. Your virtual-reality, life-movie 'world' has only virtual-reality 'people' in it. If any of us exist, we are out here. Still, our thoughts and feelings have always been beyond the reach of your senses, so why deny them now? It is really a question of discovering how you have *been* getting your thoughts about us, our thoughts, our feelings, etc.

You have several choices. We who take the path of science first put our faith in all types of thoughtless, hence impersonal!, **mechanisms**: light reflected to eyes, sound waves propagated to ears, etc., and impulses to our skull-imprisoned brain. That route, as Berkeley (if he ever lived) showed, is a dead-end. It leaves us only two viable choices. This dazzling sensory show, so life-like that most will not entertain the possibility that it is only a show, is either from a **Person** or Persons whose power, intelligence, and ingenuity dwarf ours, even though our ability to understand the full breadth of the contrast shows colossal intelligence. Or it is an unintended effect from a mindless, hence! goal-less, **will**, energy, force... The thought's the thing, not the (non)name. Take **my word**, there's only one third option: **nothing**'s out here. If you take that word—anyone's word—for anything, make sure it's from a person who is conscious of the words and of the thoughts meant. Recall all that I have told you earlier, and do not mis-take these ink marks, the light, or your brain for me.

Meditate on the option which I!, thru these words!, offer you: all these thoughts are from God who, this very moment, knows you completely the way the *N.Y. Times* article suggests your brain reads your wishes. The idea of God speaking was abroad, we are told!, long before science began. How did it get there? Imagine that in

God's Game of Wits, the final move is realizing that we have been dealing with God from the beginning. Here is a way to make that final move: **meditate** on persons, their faces, and their thoughts. What is a person's face? Even if naive belief in real faces were true, would a face be evidents for a person? Look at your face in the mirror. Concentrate, however, not on what is here in the mirror, but on you 'back there,' looking out from the eyes in your head which sits atop the shoulders from which your body extends down to your feet on the floor. Ask someone else to put her/his head next to yours. Now, two faces in the mirror. Which is yours? Which has your thoughts behind it? The following thoughts for instance. Is that my face? Only a mirror-image of it? Only a non-existent illusion 'made up' of light? Retinal images in my eyes? A flurry of neuronal activity inside my pitch-dark cranium. Or...

Is a face evidents for a person? For thoughts? What is behind the second mirror'd face? Imagine it's Descartes' face. Meditate on his thesis that a person is a spirit-being distinct from the face and the brain behind it. Pursue that thesis. Persons and thoughts can never be seen or pictured. All we can do is understand thoughts about them. (Believers often yearn to see God face to face, but whatever you'd see would not be God, though you can understand thoughts about God and God's thoughts.) So, which are better clues? A face? Words? Do either exist? P.S. Ever ask what you'd know, without words, about the role of your never-sensed brain? Words?!

Go to the library, find more 'words' like these to help you explore your options, and decide which you will assent to. While there, pull down Augustine's *De Magistro* (On the Teacher). His words will tell you what Plato's sun (*Republic*) and Aquinas' light of the agent intellect (*Summa Theologica*) are symbols for: not a mechanism, but a Person. They will tell you that God, within you, is even now trying to coach you as to which options are true. A pleasureable thought! From God. Now.

0110. WHO, NOT WHAT, IS BEHIND THE VOICE?

One shock beyond Descartes'. Descartes' *Meditations* are among the world's great literary and rhetorical masterpieces. He deliberately set out to create a mood of total and absolute doubt. Not doubt just about God's existence or the soul's immortality. And not just about minor items, e.g., whether Shakespeare's plays were composed by Bacon or Bacon's treatises by Shakespeare, which whoever ponders "What's in a name?" can discover is a question about whether those are two odd names for one person (who could be called "X" without changing anything but our calling-habits) with one history or two names for two Xs with two Ys. He doubted everything.

Almost. Descartes never explicitly extended his doubt to the people he hoped would read the *Meditations* he labored over. He explicitly extended it to his own existence, his own nature, God's and the physical world's existence and their essential natures. He carefully sketched a resolution for his doubts about those items. In addition to the thoughts whose truth or falsity he wonders about, he decides that he is most certain of his own existence, and then most certain that he is essentially a thinking being who understands thoughts and wonders how to sort out the true from the false ones, that his thoughts about God cannot come from any other source than an infinitely perfect being deserving of a special name, "Deus" or "Dieu" ("What's in a name?" applies here; Descartes did not speak or write english), and that physical or extended bodies must exist because, in effect, God assures him that they do. But he never explicitly asked the question, "Is there anyone out there to read my book?"

In fact, it was not till years after Descartes' *Meditations* had been picked over by both converts and critics that people* finally got around to the problem known in english as the problem of 'other minds' (a bow toward Descartes) and to asking *the question jealous lovers, jurors, etc., face everyday:* "What do I know about him/her?" Kant, later said it was a scandal that no one, not even Descartes, had given a really decent proof that the (physical) world existed, and Heidegger in this century said it was a scandal that anyone, Kant included, had ever thought the world was in need of (more) proof. Today's library-goer who compares them can easily see that Descartes is the one whose questions and answers are most clear and distinct. Kant expressed his inconsistent conclusions in often obscure ways which is why every good library offers contradictory expert opinions about what Kant's opinions really were. As for Heidegger... But none of the three, if they ever existed, addressed the question of other human persons* the way it must be addressed in connection with the question of persons who are more than human, i.e., divine. (*The best introduction to these discussions is the first of M.Gardner's *The Whys of a Philosophical Scrivener*.)

Drama often helps us capture essential moods. That is why Descartes, in his first meditation, starts off with dramatic fiction. He writes it as if it is a diary entry. He has reached a point in life, he says, where he knows his mind is filled with a Babel of contradictory opinions. Those who read this with his *Discourse on Method* behind them know he had an excellent college education, which meant he'd been exposed to thousands of facts and dozens of ways to interpret them, and that he also had a lively and varied post-college life of travel and study. Today, he says, he has decided to carry out a long-postponed obligation, namely, to sit down and decide just which of all the things he has learned are really true. The disadvantage most students have in getting the full impact of Descartes' opening meditation is that, unlike him, they are not as knowledgeable about physics and physiology. Or not as courageous as Descartes in confronting the fact that, if physics and brain science are true, then naive realism is false. It is false that what you see is a book, what you feel are hands, etc. You have no direct link to any physical object. *Not unless it's your own brain.* It's the one physical thing your present sense-data, feelings, memory-images, and thoughts most extensively 'correlate with.' It is also—and this is one of God's most ingenious tricks—the part of your body you will never feel or sense in any way whatsoever! And, if the physical-bodies half of 'nature' does not exist or if it contains no bodies larger than subatoms, brains do not exist. (A fact that is crucial for takers of Sherlock Holmes' "exclude what's impossible" advice.) The ancients believed they could prove the existence of a less-provable God from a more-provable external 'nature.' Descartes was the first to successfully decipher the clues: *We can't prove God by those things, because we can't prove them except by God.*

A parenthesis? Typical of the library evidence I count on is the following. First is a century-old quote from William James' *The Principles of Psychology* (1890):

> **The 'entire brain-process' is not a physical fact at all**. It is the appearance to an onlooking mind of a multitude of physical facts. 'Entire brain' is nothing but our name for the way in which a million of molecules arranged in certain positions may affect our sense. On the principles of the corpuscular or mechanical philosophy, the only realities are the separate molecules, or at most the cells. Their aggregation into a 'brain' is a fiction of popular speech. Such a fiction cannot serve as the objectively real counterpart to any psychic state whatever. Only a genuinely physical fact can so serve. But the molecular fact is the only genuine physical fact... (Ch.VI)

James later moved the passage from that obscure position to one of prominence in the epilogue to *Psychology: Briefer Course*. In the 15th of his *Talks to Teachers* he added "I cannot see how such a thing as our consciousness can possibly be produced by a nervous machinery." James' judgment about brain-claims has been confirmed over and over during the present century. In 1979, Richard Restak wrote:

> Brain scientists... have demonstrated that neurons in reality are separate cells that communicate with each other but are never in direct physical contact. This rules out the view that nerve impulses travel through

the brain like water through a system of pipes. (*The Brain: The Last Frontier*, chapter 9)

Be cautious when reading about the brain. That is, while you gear up to put on the genuinely scientific mindset so brilliantly dramatized by Descartes, you must get in the habit of doing two things. First, being alert to Disney-like anthropomorphizing. 'Brain-talk' is saturated with fantasies about unconscious neurons 'communicating' with one another by sending 'neurotransmitter' chemical-grams imagined to be carrying 'information' and 'data'! And keeping in mind the physics that proves that brains do not exist. **Not even neurons!** Dip extensively into the literature on nuclear or atomic physics, in order to see why James' reference to millions of brain-cells (neurons) should be translated into a reference to zillions of molecules, then into a reference to zillions of atoms, and then into thoughts about subatoms which, <u>if</u> they exist, are the <u>only</u> bodies that exist and which, <u>if</u> they exist, do <u>not</u> 'make up' anything, not even solar-system-like atoms, except in our imaginations or thoughts:

The [empty] space in the atom outside the nucleus is enormous compared with the size of the nucleus, or with the much smaller size of the electron. In the atom of hydrogen the single electron is near the outer rim of the atom. If its nucleus were enlarged to the size of a baseball, its electron would be a speck about eight city blocks away. Actually, of course, this atomic distance is small. The diameter of a hydrogen atom is nearly 1/200,000,000 of an inch; in other words, 200,000,000 hydrogen atoms could be placed one next to the other in an inch. Relative to the nucleus or to the electron, however, the [empty] space is prodigious. (S.Hecht, *Explaining the Atom*, III, 4)

Incidentally, anthropomorphism is rampant everywhere. Among the evolutionary biologists who believe as fervently in such imaginary agents as 'natural selection' and the 'evolutionary process' as primitives believed in ghosts. And among those physicists who assume the reality of unseen forces as nonchalantly as they assume the reality of unseen bodies allegedly pumping out those forces which then leap across empty space to push or pull other bodies, distant and unseen. Actually...

The words "attract" and "pull", which we used in the last example, are dangerous words. They suggest an analogy with certain psychological experiences. We are attracted by objects we desire, like food or a late-model car; and we like to imagine the attraction of bodies by the earth as the satisfaction of a sort of desire, at least on the side of the earth. But such an interpretation would be what the logician calls an *anthropomorphism*, that is, the assignment of human qualities to physical objects... When we say that Newton's law of attraction explains the falling of bodies, we mean that the movement of bodies toward the earth is *incorporated into a general **law*** according to which all bodies move towards each other. The word "attraction" as employed by Newton means no more than such a movement of bodies toward each other. (H.Reichenbach, *The Rise of Scientific Philosophy*, ch.1; emphasis added.)

Only if students of the future are properly instructed in the true implications of scientific hypotheses, i.e., guesses, about the never-experienced physical universe, will they be ready to experience the shock of Descartes' question, "Do physical things exist?", and the shock of Kant's answer, "If physics is viewed as guesses about things in themselves, i.e., independent of mind, it rests on faith as much as theology does." And ready for the more ultimate issues. William Barrett took it as a frivolity that Russell took questions like Einstein's "Is the moon there when no one's looking?" seriously. In Chapter 9 of *The Illusion of Technique*, he repeats Russell's story about the day the latter went to class to prove the 'external' (physical) world but, realizing the proof was faulty, decided to prove "that there was no good reason to think anything except myself existed." Anyone who does not know why Russell saw this solipsist question as the inescapable challenge of modern physical and physiological theories is not educated well enough to get to the bottom of the ethical or moral problem today's world is faced with: If God is dead, then why *oughtn't* the strongest humans to exert their might for any purpose they choose? Barrett, for years, touted Heidegger, which partly explains his reaction to Russell. But later (1986), in *Death of the Soul* (thought to be geared to students and lay readers but especially important for re-thinking academics), he confessed that "there is a certain desolate and empty quality about his thought," to which soul-less emptiness Barrett ascribes Heidegger's lack of an ethics. **Enough for this parenthesis; back to work.**

Fiction? Did you ever notice that a prominent newspapaper does not divide best-sellers into "Truth" and "Fiction," but into "Fiction" and "Non-Fiction"? Descartes wanted to know the truth, but modern thinkers have more and more shied away from the quest for certainty about the truth. As opposed to certainty about 'facts' [sic]. No layperson would dream of imitating 'scientists' who claim that evolution is a fact, but who then redefine "fact" to mean "a widely-held and well-supported guess that may in the future turn out to be false," because laypeople know that "fact" normally means what is true, and what is later discovered (truly!) to be false never was true, hence never was a fact. You do understand this, ~~balciatlea x#% lbuter?@ 1a2b3c4dxolwyjf~~ (sorry, my brain [or was it yours?] momentarily went crazy, so let's try again) even if you decide none of it is true, right? You can't judge the truth or falseness of thoughts or opinions you don't ~~gh*&~~ understand, can you?

The best way to introduce the bottom-line thesis of these (non)pages—cues and clues for your future meditations—is to return to the fact that Descartes' *Meditations* are presented in the guise of an obviously untrue situation. He was not sitting down and writing out a diary entry for himself. In Discourse IV, published in 1637, he outlined the argument which he simply expanded into the six meditations that he published four years later. Fact? Fiction? If not everything called "fact" is true, then maybe not everything called "fiction" is false. Before me lies *Rashomon: a film by Akira Kurosawa*, which actually looks like a book, not a film. I didn't read it, but I saw it? on late-night TV around 1959. The book? says that the movie was partly based on a short story which "took an old melodrama" and made it "ask Pilate's question." Which prompts me to tell you that the story is mainly true. God did, in fact, create six people in medieval Japan whose paths crossed just the way the movie depicts. One, a warrior, was killed. The question was "By whom and why?" Four different people told four different stories. But, if there is only one world, they could not all be true in every detail, so who was telling the truth? (Each account might be true about parts of the drama but wrong about others.) Two other players are a priest and a commoner. When the priest learns that the dead warrior's story—told through a medium—is contradicted by a woodsman who saw it all, the priest is unconvinced, because dead men are not sinful enough to lie. The commoner, tho, shrugs off the problem: "Who's honest nowadays?" Stop. Where are those last words from? A medieval Japanese? A melodrama-teller? A short story writer? Kurosawa? Me? This computer? This book? This page? Your brain? Or God? If the world holds all those things, which of them did you just see? What's the truth?

Let the commoner in the movie represent the student in the library. And let us assume that, in the library as opposed to the movie (book? text? your imagination?), the authors of the thousands of claims and counterclaims are honest. The student's question becomes, not "Who's honest nowadays?", but "Who's right nowadays?" Whoever wants the truth, the whole truth, and nothing but the truth should be thought of as someone who wants to create an inner model of history which has all the details right. Did the paths of six imaginary! people cross as reported? Were there two people in 1600, one named Francis Bacon and one named William Shakespeare? Did one of them write two sets of works? Did ancient Hebrews believe the earth is flat? Did Copernicus think it was a sphere at the universe's center? Did Ptolemy think the sun was? Agree or not, do you understand the thoughts that have been coming to you? If so, see whether you understand this: **You have had to learn for yourself every last fact you know** about Descartes, Kant, Gardner, Barrett, Russell, Kurosawa, God, your brain, ancient Hebrews, Ptolicus, and Copernemy. And—unless you are not like me—you would not know a single thing about any of those people or facts, **were it not for what APPEAR! TO BE words, words, and more words**.

The thought that just came to you will require a great deal of stop-to-think'ing. But on it rests the entire belief-system now being proposed to you. You can respond to it in any way you choose: ignore it, assent to it, assent to some and reject the rest, just ignore it, wonder some more about it, ignore it, etc. The phrase "appears to be" is, of course, crucial. What you mis-take for words are parts of your TVFs, created exactly the same way the titles and credits on what appears to be the movie- or TV-screen are created, what you see 'conjures' whole modules of associated memory-imagery in exactly the same way that other patterned colors 'conjure' associated-images, the thoughts coming to you now are being created exactly the same way every thought you've ever had has been created. How? Among the impossible answers that must be excluded is this: these thoughts are coming from a human person who guided his brain to guide his fingers to strike about sixty keys in various sequences to produce a 'lot' of pieces of paper covered with sequenced ink-mark ciphers which have since then been transported through space to your hands where they are now reflecting light to your retinas which is triggering impulses that are travelling via your optic nerves to your brain where the 'information' they carry is being interpreted by your brain which, like a superpowerful computer, holds billions of gigabites of data from prior input which has been catalogued the way brains with human, as distinct from brains with cat or frog, hardwiring (see Restak's sixth chapter), etc., etc. That's naive. The initially improbable truth is that...

VIA YOUR THOUGHTS, GOD IS DEALING DIRECTLY WITH YOU.

Talking to you, if you like. Making proposals that you are left free to adopt, reject, put on hold, and so on. That conclusion is reached by following Sherlock's advice, "**Exclude the impossible**, and whatever remains, however improbable [at first], must be the truth." No other cause is capable of producing thoughts. Certainly no other cause can produce thoughts about all of space and time, productions so clearly divine that they are regularly called "God's-eye views." Such God's-eye views can come from no **body**, certainly! What unsensed, unconscious, and isolated neuro**n** or neuron**s** is/are sending up these proposals into your non-unconscious? And God's-eye views can come from no **person** except a divine one who is now prepared to reveal, to any who have the time and the opportunity (we call compulsory education what Aristotle viewed as leisure), how all the pieces of the puzzle fit together correctly. In general. **Basic**-ally. After noticing, and then ridding ourselves of, the current clutter of myths and fictions. Beginning with language and brains.

Laws. Descartes recoiled from the thought that all his errors came from God. But those who now realize that the text of *Genesis 1* and *Josua 10* led many literal-minded believers into error should be better prepared to realize that God not only can but does deceive. Directly. Just as God also reveals truth. Directly. Jeremiah (if he lived) or God (if God exists) tells us in 31:33-4 "I will place my law within them, and write it upon their hearts; I will be their God, and they shall be my people. No longer will they have need to teach their friends and kinsmen how to know the Lord," though the telling was/is in Hebrew. Long years later, an inspired Thomas Jefferson repeated that same democratic idea, this time in english:

> He who made us would have been a pitiful bungler if he had made the rules of moral conduct a matter of science [learned only in college]. For one man of science, there are a thousand who are not. Man was destined for society. His morality therefore was to be formed to this object. He was endowed with a sense of right and wrong merely relative to this. This sense is as much a part of his nature as the sense of hearing, seeing, feeling; it is the true foundation of morality. (Letter to Peter Carr, 1787)

There are rules to God's Game of Wits. One—call it "the consensus-appeal rule"—is so obvious that today's experts have naively* come to rely on it as an adequate test for truth: if (we believe) most of our peers agree on something, we feel a tug (from God) to agree with them. Unless he was a figment of imagination, C.S. Lewis dug up evidence to support Jefferson's claim: some form of the Golden Rule—which, according to Saint Paul, implicitly contains the entire moral law—was revealed to those who shaped each of the major cultures [sic] of which we have a record. That reassures us that being moral is a duty. But God does not make such revelations by tucking genes into ancestral DNA or innate ideas into our souls or properties into fictitious essences or natures. God does it directly, e.g., each time the still, small 'voice of conscience' speaks to us. (*What if the stadium is dark and deserted?)

God also offers doubts to tug us toward <u>dis</u>agreeing with popular opinion when the time comes for us to engage in the 'examined life.' Doubt is often a prelude toward another moment of divine revelation of truth that goes beyond, or even shows to be false, opinions till then mis-taken for truth. Which is why J.S.Mill and we tolerate doubt-raising dissent. We take it for granted that the honestly-erring—those, both theists and atheists, who seek the truth with diligence and good-willed honesty—are to be viewed, not only as not morally wrong, but often—when measured by the yardstick for moral character—as praiseworthy. So much is clear to those of us who enjoy recognition for our well-intentioned efforts. The coin's other side is equally clear. Being closed-minded and refusing to honestly seek the truth, can be a grave sin. Especially when—in 1995—scientific revelations about the laws of physics and chemistry make it clear that God is prepared to respond favorably to our decisions to bring mass death and destruction on those whom we choose to attack as enemies.

The laws of sensation, especially, are part of God's Game of Wits. God is the one in charge of everything. Contrary to appearances, bodies have no power.

Hence God, not matter, conveys the felt effects of our benevolence or hostility to one another. But norm-ally in accordance with the general 'norms of nature' which can be found 'in' our streams of sense-data, which norms allow us to predict what we'll **probably** sense next. The idea is simple. While in your naive-realist mood, get in the habit of studying movie (and TV!) screens and the way sounds accompany them. You can tell when a 'plane' is going away from you ('its' colors take up less and less of the steady-sized screen) or coming closer ('its' colors take up more and more), you can guess when it has crashed even if it is off-screen (a well-timed sound comes from the speakers), and so on. Tacitly relying on your vast memory of past sensation-sequences, you instantly recognize it if something's wrong with the color projector or the sound system: when the two are out of synch (you hear the heroine's 'words' either before or after her 'lips' move), when the film is being run backwards, when crude trick photography is being used, and so on. Obviously, the colors do not cause the sounds or vice-versa, but both are caused by unseen and unheard mechanisms. Then use that study to discover how completely your TVF-color-seeing and sound-hearing—when feels, tastes, and odors are added—parallel movie-going. Finally, by 'dipping into' their words, words, and more meditation-cuing (non) words, discover how Berkeley and Hume showed Kant where Descartes' thinking about sensing was deficient. And understand why James was stretching the truth (a lot!) when, in lecture three of *Pragmatism*, he said that "Berkeley does n't deny matter, then; he simply tells us what it consists of. It is a true name for just so much in the way of sensations." Another—later—Harvard 'pragmatist' named W.Quine, put it better:

> As an empiricist I continue to think of the conceptual scheme of science as a tool, ultimately, for predicting future experience in the light of past experience. Physical objects are conceptually imported into the situation as convenient intermediaries—not by definition in terms of experience, but simply as irreducible posits comparable, epistemologically, to the gods of Homer. For my part I do, qua lay physicist, believe in physical objects and not in Homer's gods; and I consider it a scientific error to believe otherwise. But in point of epistemological footing the physical objects and the gods differ only in degree and not in kind. Both sorts of entities enter our conception only as cultural posits. The myth of physical objects is epistemologically superior to most in that it has proved much more efficacious than other myths as a device for working a manageable structure into the flux of experience. ("Two Dogmas of Empiricism," 1953)

Be clear about the link between laws and what exists. Laws as such don't exist. "Oh, doesn't the law of inertia say 'All bodies stay put or move straight ahead at a steady pace when nothing is preventing it'?" No, laws don't speak. Or govern. 'Laws' are not out there. **We predict what we hope things will keep doing in the future, based on what we remember them doing in the past**. Things, not laws, do or act. If bodies larger than subatoms are mythical, then stars, planets, cannon balls, etc., have never done anything. If only subatoms exist, then only they move, and, by zooming in close (always in imagination), we discover that their motions are complex beyond description. How about this: "For the cesium-133 atoms in most atomic clocks, the frequency is 9,192,631,770 vibrations per second" (*Time*, 1-13-92, p.53)? Or: "In less time than it takes to say 'off-off-Broadway', a two-atom molecule such as iodine can perform about 10 billion rotations" (*Science News*, 3-3-90, p.135)? The library is full of such descriptions. Which are all unprovable facts suggested by God. The physical-universe story is a small bit of self-revelation by a God whose creative imagination dwarfs those God created: Shakespeare's, Einstein's, and Jonathan Harrison's.

God's motives? If it makes no sense to speak of physical laws *as such* if nothing physical exists, or of biological laws if nothing biologically alive exists, or of neurological laws if no brains exist, or of psychological laws if no psyches exist, then it makes no sense to speak of other people's motives if other persons do not exist. If you are alone in the universe, then your motives are the only ones. If you freely choose to believe that matter or a blind energy called "will" is the 'god' behind your life-movie, or if, like Einstein, you freely choose to regard the 'laws of nature' as if they are so real and so awesome that they deserve to be called "God," then it will make no sense for you to inquire into your god's motives. Only if you freely choose (you don't feel like a victim of a compulsion neurosis or psychosis here, do you?) to believe that the wizard behind the scenes is a lot of Homeric gods or the one Hebrew deity, will it make sense to ask "Why is God so good to me?" or, as God tempts so many to ask, "Why is God so cruel?" Agree with Quine, and these final questions boil down to the one which the great Hebrew thinkers wrestled with: "Why?" For those who give the majority answer when asked "What is your religion?", the question becomes even more acute when they pray the "Lead us not into temptation" petition of their Lord's prayer and mean it the way it must be meant, literally. Truth is best served by calling "a spade" whatever spades exist. Why pain? Temptation? Why pleasure?!

Why does God stay behind the scenes? It's obviously part of a plan to make us free to believe what we will. In the course of our late-1900's educations, we are offered dozens of pseudo-causes in place of God. When I was very young, I **believed** that it made perfect sense to pray for sunny weather if a picnic was planned or for rain if our garden languished. Later on I embraced a Laplace-like, determinist **faith** that tomorrow's weather is already in today's cards and that only a lack of information prevents forecasters from being infallible. My prayers had asked for miracles, for interventions in the norm-al course of things. But those days of thinking that God intervenes, and only occasionally, are long past. Just as long past as the days when I thought God, from a place high above space and time, saw the past, present, and future in themselves (absurd!, because that would mean God sees me as I was but am not, sees me as I will be but am not, and also sees me as I am, which is the only one of me there is!), when I thought God created a universe-ful of things which, once created, acted in virtue of their inner phusis or nature (as if the moon has an infinite, built-in supply of 'inertial' energy that can keep it moving forever!, as if slit-split photons 'know' what their partners are doing!), and when I imagined God merely stood by and 'permitted' pain and suffering to occur. Now I **know** that God proposed the truth via C.J.S. and O.F. that God 'hand-moves' every subatom and "flawlessly orchestrates" their dances with the creation of sense-data, etc. So, if a temptation—to error or to sin—comes, it's not from a brain but directly from God. And if, as a result of one person's sinful decision, pain is felt by another, God and not matter is the conduit. Just as we are not a blind and deaf Gaia's eyes and ears, so too **we are not God's hands and not channels of grace from God to others.** God gives both the impetus to good directly to one, and—when the response is favorable—the grace directly to the other. That's what ~~this quintuplist theory~~ no, I no, God! is proposing to you. Right this instant. For your free response. Favorable or not. Got all that? (It's a lot to get! A God's-eye view. A huge effect to seek the cause of.)

In other words, God—while remaining behind the appearances—has been dropping clues all along to lead inquiring minds to the truth. **Quantum laws in physics and bell-curve statistics in psychology are the final clues**, obviously designed to convince us that a free, chaos-avoiding Person, not some mind-less forces or laws (physics) and not any fictitious nature or nurture (psychology), must be behind our private life-movies. And, just as truly as we non-geniuses can comprehend enough to be in awe of the humans we call "walking encyclopedias," we can comprehend enough of the divine productions to stand in awe of the Divine Producer whose ways are not so hopelessly above ours as we've been told. Next spring, for instance, spend your leisure studying maple leaves. Use naive-realism and the old protoplasm concept. Watch how, as if from nowhere, protoplasm pushes out from each winter-barren twig. Only it does so, not in the form of dripping ooze, but as if it is being delicately molded according to a single *general* plan into separate leaves. Then, try to find two leaves that are exactly alike, down to the last atom. Meditate on those atoms. Every one is like a mini-solar-system whose dancing planets must be kept in place by an unseen hand. (Do you really believe in shells, orbit-paths thru the ether, etc.?! Or, for that matter, in invisible hands? Recall those playing cards moved by invisible, rule-following card-players.) Why does God make it easier to believe in atoms and quantum laws than to adopt this final revelation? One of God's most important motives must be to make us free to believe—and to love—as we will.

Other motives? God clearly wants to bind us to each other. Start meditating with the old time-fiction: the time before creation. Put yourself in God's place. There's no one to help you. You have to do it all. Suppose what we call "God" is actually a triumvirate who enjoy one another's company. They share with us the pleasure of personal achievement, but they also want us to be in some measure responsible for one another's pleasure. If you ask Dad to give you the car keys, he could give you the keys immediately. But if Dad says "If your mom says it's alright, I will," whom do you thank? Especially if mom's "Alright" means one of three things for her: a bit of pleasure foregone, an added effort made, some pain endured. If you meditate long and hard on these and other hints and connect them with what is entailed in following the Golden Rule's bidding, you will go far toward understanding God.

Intellectual virtues or habits. Hume rejected naive realism as unequivocally as any one: "This universal and primary opinion of all men is soon destroyed by the slightest philosophy" he wrote in sec.XII of his first *Enquiry*. A few pages later, in a footnote, he retreated to that universal opinion by rejecting the obvious alternative, saying that Berkeley's arguments "admit of no answer and produce no conviction," adding "their only effect is to cause [...] momentary amazement and irresolution and confusion." But Hume was confessing, not legislating, as is clear from the fact that Berkeley was never irresolute and never felt as confused as Hume admitted in his *Treatise* that he (Hume) often was. In a sense, tho, he was right. Whoever isn't amazed, not just momentarily but permanently, has not yet understood. Test yourself.

Look into another person's eyes and say "I know what I see isn't you but only part of my private life-movie"! (Each time the sensation of crossing your eyes is followed by one 'face' becoming two in your TVF, though, the improbable will seem a little less impossible.)

Academics, who favor skepticism to dogmatists' intolerance, prefer to dodge these issues. Why? The best answer is "Habit!" God-taught naive-realism and Newton-taught exclusion of God from physics, physiology, and psychology textbooks, **along with our tolerance for treating fictions as realities**, are habits. Like sociologists, James understood that such habits are "the fly-wheel of society." The in-attentive—not un-conscious!—student stands when asked, but balks at lying down. X'ans are taught "That land is our land," though Y'ans are assured from youth that "It's ours!" In a word, thoughts and sentiments are proposed by God along the lines of the law of habit: "Twenty experiences shape our thoughts and feelings more than one." Naive-realist and cultural thought-experiences add up to far more than just twenty. Ignore the proposals of these pages and your old thought-habits will never change. Such naiveté and ignorance: are they moral vices? Maybe not in the past. But the world can no longer afford their pain-occasioning consequences.

PREFACE THREE

What follows next is an alternate Sixth Re-Meditation*. Out in Ohio, I made many notes, mental and otherwise, for a new sixth chapter to replace the original. Then I reviewed the original and decided it was not as unsuccessful as I'd feared. (*The focus of both is on voices. Of the 'things being told to you' via these 'words,' whose voice is the source?)

Still, some key points were underplayed, so...

It is exactly midnight, between June 18 and 19. I spent today?-yesterday? writing the alternative that follows (this is a post- not a pre-face). Since I like both versions, I am going to include both and let you make the decision as to which you will regard as the real, true, genuine sixth and call "Remeditation 0110." What you hold in your hands will not change, no matter what you decide to call it. That, of course, is part of the major proposal here: your imagination is stocked with incompatible interpretation-systems, and deciding the truth about the world is to be viewed as selecting the right overall system and then trying to make sure all its details are as accurate as possible. In Freudian terms, your grand-theory decision is deciding what is false projecting* and what is understanding what is really going on. Freud decided wrongly that those who believe in God seize their picture of Dad and expand it into an illusory Big Daddy in the Sky. In fact, he seized the bundle-of-perceptions image of a thinker ("mind"), stripped it of consciousness, and wrote myth-filled books about a mythical Unconscious (Mind). There. You have two proposals. Take your choice. (*Don't like projection? Try attribution. Imposition? Theory-laden perception? Or...)

The choice of God or Unconscious is different from taking your choice on 'speaking' Centigrade or Fahrenheit. The true parallel to the first choice is what you choose to believe you are applying the alternate C-or-F 'languages' to: air temperature, kinetic motion of molecules, felt heat and cold (sense-data), etc. Similarly, choosing one, I, or 0001, or six, 6, or 0110, is not crucial, but whether the numbers allegedly named by them exist or not is. And whether you call what follows a remeditation, a chapter, a section of a singel GUTE, a segment of a single proposal, isn't, but what it is you are calling is. It is not important whether you decide that a total-sense-changing "no" in Chapter I, Eight, regarding Hume, is a misprint or a deliberate temptation, but deciding which of the two resulting senses captures the truth is. Every interpretation is an interpretation, but not everything you apply an interpretation to is an interpretation, even though you may choose to interpret it as if it is.

So... Do you partly interpret everything except God as having God for its original designer? Or do you choose to interpret your experience as part of a universe that is without any planning and creative God? Compare the universe to... this text? Was it planned or not? What evidence will you use to decide?

0110-B. VOICES, THE SCIENTIFIC TRUTH ABOUT.

[**An aside.** Why is it possible for reasoners to follow a syllogism when one premise is cut off from the second by an 'aside' like this one? Well, why can an **entire system** get built up over the course of a lifetime, even though dreamless sleep by definition brings to a halt all conscious linking as utterly as Lucretius thought death did (headstones do say "Here sleeps..."), and even though sleep-time dreams inject all kinds of absurd counter-propositions between the premises? Because the steady-state system is the backdrop for the awake-times. Asides cue thoughts just as orderly presentations do, zoom us into some location in the system (note where god, unlike dog, takes you), invite us to see new things, change old ones, etc., but are less lengthy. In both cases, we race right along, when the cues and their sequences are familiar; quando non—e.g., nihil in intellectu nisi prius in sensu—we work harder. Taken any naps since you read page i? Had any crazy dreams? Any (difficilior) fugue states? **End.**]

Where are you? Sabbath, June 3, 1995, 5:20am. Sabbath? (Look it up.) What day and date is it in the

139

universe? Really? (Where did the 5th to the 14th of October go in 1582 when the Gregorian calendar replaced the Julian?) You are trying to decide ~~what's true~~ which thoughts are true (that's better; how much unclued rewordking has gone into this!). Since you picked up this book, thought after thought has come to you. From that perspective, the best way to say 'where you are' is this: you are making decisions about their truth. You are concentrating on sifting the true from the false. Sifting true thoughts from false ones. From that perspective, your present attaches right to your past: all sorts of thoughts have been coming to you over the course of your lifetime, and you have been routinely keeping some, rejecting others, and putting others on hold. Like my earlier *Meditations*, these *Re-Meditations* invite you to make some radical alterations in your earliest beliefs. Or, if you have made some but they are the wrong ones, they invite you to re-alter them. Or, if they were the right ones, they invite you to keep them. So, where do you stand now?

[**Another.** Whose voice have you been listening to? Asking that question is the counterpart to asking myself whose ears will be doing the listening. For all I know, you may not even exist as of this date. Or, like me, you may have been part of this universe for a long time and are in the midst of a post-1995 life-cycle. I.Berlin, from whose words I learned (in my present life) that my first discovery of the sense-datum theory was not the first, was interviewed by S.Cassidy:

Philosophical questions, he said, no longer kept him awake at night. "But those ideas gripped me. When an idea is fascinating, bad or good, right or wrong, I'm interested. I want to know where that idea comes from."

Great thinkers "of the not-too-distant past," he said, are so alive to him that "I think I hear them talk. It's an illusion, but unless I think I hear their voices, I'm not under the impression that I understand their thoughts."

"At the end of my life," he said, smiling, "I want to know more than I did at the beginning. And I couldn't get that from philosophy." (3-24-91 *N.Y. Times Book Review*)

As you ran your eyes across those rows and rose, did you hear a distinctive voice? Hers? (She was doing the reporting.) His? (He was being quoted.) Mine? (I made the whole thing up.) Change "I want to know where that idea comes from" to "I want to know where that voice comes from," and it will take you right back to page i. Related to all this, remember how Roxanne misidentified a source? **End.**]

Individual persons: which of us do you know best? I admit I am not 100% positive that I wrote the *Meditations*. I think the first time it ever occurred to me was when someone I taught told me that he was once asked if Descartes had been his teacher. Is it possible, though? When I was younger, I would have said "Absolutely not." I was taught that reincarnation is a heresy. Since flesh as such does not exist, though, not even incarnation (interpreted naive realistically) is possible. Which raises the old question, What makes one person distinct from another? If there is nothing to differentiate two things, then there can't be two, only one with two names. Aquinas, whose GUTE I began to absorb at the age of twenty-one, taught that humans are distinguished by the matter-component of their make-up, whereas immaterial persons like angels have to be distinguished by their essences. That is why countless humans with the same! essence can belong to the one human species, and why each angel is the one and only individual in his(?) species. But, when Descartes or I declared that humans have no essential relation to their material bodies, ~~we~~ he or! I paved the way for Locke and others to reopen the question. Locke mistakenly decided that different memories are what make persons different. That was nearly as foolish as thinking that a newborn human is not already what it is before it receives its name. A person must be, in order to think and, by the same token, in order to acquire memories.

Rule: Do not abandon commonsense entirely! There is nothing I am more absolutely sure of than the fact that it is I and no one else who is doing this thinking. So, whether or not Aquinas, Locke, or anyone can explain how or why pristine-state humans differ, it doesn't change the fact that we do. One of the most ingenious features of God's Game of Wits is the fact that, although all questions grow out of our original set of beliefs described here as "good commonsense," so many individual beliefs in that set are originally 'tacit,' that is, so much taken-for-granted that we never notice them. (Write down the three things you would put at the top of a list of "What is absolutely necessary for me to be as happy as possible.") No one who did not already have a solid 'sense of self' would know who "Who are you?" is being directed to. Though I've only been able to read him during my current life, I like the advice Whitehead gave: our task is to satisfy commonsense. Which I take to mean we must be sure our 'professional' theory is consistent with the true basics of our God-given commonsense. Which is why I also know I exist: non-existing beings don't think, make mistakes, learn the truth, or withhold assent on anything.

It's your turn now. Do you exist? The belief that you do! needs no other proof than this fact: it is a thread so long and so thoroughly woven into the entire fabric of your everyday belief-system that the latter will unravel into schizophrenia, multiple-personality, or even worse forms of dementia, if it is removed. What it needs is recognition. The type that psychologists like Erik Erikson have tried to inject into the psychoanalytic tradition. Or, better, the type that Descartes captured with his superb meditations. For those who subscribe to Mencken's "One horse-laugh is worth ten thousand syllogisms," gobs of commonsense help reinforce the point. If you came out of a bomb-shelter after every human but one had been killed, would you wonder which one it was? Is it possible that every last human died from simultaneous heart attacks twenty minutes ago? If you were a watchperson closing up at midnite, found the door to my dark office open, and called "Yoohoo, anybody in there?", would you take my "Nope, nobody in here" word for it? So, yoohoo. Anybody there?

Rule: Do not abandon commonsense talk entirely. Not when it is far better than theoretical substitution. For instance, do not get in the bad habit of using "my soul (or mind, will, etc.)" instead of "I." Or of imagining that "imagine" is not a perfectly good substitute for "think." Imag**in**ing is not imaging. It is thinking. Imagining can be understanding what someone tells you. Imagine that that's what I am telling you. What I am proposing to you. Will you assent to that proposal? Understanding is **MORE** than sensing which is more than imaging. So, too, is imag**in**ing, whether it is imagining what might have happened, or imagining what might be going on, or imagining what will happen, or imagining what didn't, can't, and won't ever take (its) place in cosmic history. Those who think what's imagined did, does, or will*, call it thinking (about the past, present, or future). Or remembering, knowing, or foreseeing <u>that</u> such-and-such... When they aren't using non-english cues and clues! That is my personal opinion. Really, your private thoughts about what my opinion is. Your personal private thoughts. Which *you* understand, not your mind. Which *you* can freely assent to or dissent from, not your will. Which two doings *you* can do even while you, not your eyes or brain, are aware of these rows and rose that keep crossing the foveal area of your TVF. Which three you can do simultaneously with a fourth whereby <u>you</u>, not your memory, are marginally aware of oceans of imagery constantly being awakened as these rows and rose... Take the Rorty Test: assent or not, do you at least understand the proposals being sent your way? QU: Recognize the voice yet? (*Add "...take place" tacitly.)

Ockham was right. None of the proposed attempts to make everyday commonsense clearer or to justify it 'metaphysically' has succeeded at all. It is folly to think we can't be sure individuals exist until we can explain what makes them individual and how we know them. True, if all we know is that there are 5.7 billion humans today, we may know little more about most of them than "S/he is another 1*." (Till we begin constructing our inner model of outer reality, we don't even know that much about any 1.) Unless you are different, you've grown up believing you live among thousands of other people, few of whom you know or would recognize individually. "I know X" should be viewed as a generalization or as shorthand for all the things you know about X, and what James wrote home in a letter applies perfectly: "No one sees farther into a generalization than his own knowledge of details extends." He didn't add "individual" to "details." He didn't need to, do you think? (Don't answer that unless you know to whom the question is addressed.) On that score, I presume you are the individual among us you know best. If you fall in love, you will probably be able to do what most do: exchange endless details about your life with someone who will do the same, without once getting confused about who's who. (*That is synonymous with the all-important "1 MORE!")

[A warning against becoming bewitched by the semantic shell-games made possible by such terms as "same," "one," "common," and "identical." That is, against the ambiguities that formerly seduced me into firmly embracing the doctrine of universals. What made Plato resist Parmenides, Leibniz reject Spinoza, Kierkegaard attack Hegel, and all parties to take a side re the principle of individuation and the identity of indiscernibles was/is, in the final analysis, not just a solution but—at the same time—a decision. The solution is then used to justify the decision. Bookworms will see this text's adoption of the space-matrix idea at the outset, a quasi-marriage of Plato's

Timaeus and Kant's *Critique*, as part of the solution to an ancient puzzle and part of this grand unifying theory.]

The actual truth vs mere possibilities. By tying Newton's ideas about space and time to our spread-out, temporally-successive sense-data, Kant set the stage for today's talk about grand unifying theories and/or theories of everything, which talk comes from the physicists who presumably pay little or no attention to ordinary language theorists who—frustrated with monists' commonsense-denying 'grand theories'—condemn system-building. In this abridgment of a longer synopsis that runs to 601 small-type pages, there is no way to deal with all their half-, quarter-, and lesser-truths, but both the physicists and the ordinary-language species of the linguistic-turners were partly right. We **must** have a single, grand theory. For most folks, though, their everyday commonsense **is** that grand theory. Aristotle and Aquinas clarified, i.e., made explicit the most basic of common sense's tacit features. But its naive realism is a grand illusion, and only a radically-revised professional theory can incorporate both the best of everyday commonsense which places such great <u>emphasis</u> on the 'sensed world' and the real <u>truth</u> about it.

Emphasis and truth. Maybe I am Descartes, consigned to a purgatorial re-run to see whether I can improve the set of habits shorthanded as "my moral character" (the heart of being a good vs a not-good citizen), but how do I even know he ever lived? How do you know I ever lived? What's your evidence? Or mine? Portraits I've seen of Descartes are not like what I see when I look in a mirror. Nor is what I see in the mirror like what I'm told (Xtra sound 'words' of others) are baby photos of me. (I doubt I'd recognize photos of Descartes when he was a newborn.) In fact, the more I have thought about it, the clearer it's become that my 'portrait' of Descartes consists mostly of what I've learned 'thru' rows and rose of tiny black figures like these, not thru portraits of his face. (Skip what comes next if you're squeamish: how many of your closest acquaintances could you identify from photos of their bottoms? At various ages!) Still, **we do depend on all types of sense-data**, whether to know who just walked into the room (and which memory-module to call up), what s/he says, which book conveys the 'voice' of Descartes and which that of Berlin. That is what I referred to above as common sense's *emphasis* on the 'sensed world.' But, once you've discovered that naive realism is an illusion, it becomes clear that sense-data provide only *clues to possibilities* so far as the realities beyond the perimeter of your sensed 'world' are concerned. You may think you have a pretty good idea of how I—or is it Descartes in a later 'life'?—think. But what proof do *you* have that either of us ever existed? We didn't. Or that I am really I and not Descartes? I am. Which of your belief-options are true? None of them. This is the issue I? referred to earlier as the *truth* about your sensed 'world.'

[**Again.** Scientific truth does not exist. Only true thoughts do. Though you're free to mentally group all true thoughts, then shorthand them as "truth." Every would-be scientist must get in the habit of resisting the temptation to think every noun is the name for a thing. The easiest way to get in that bathi is by listing what exists and then seeing whether you can switch *from nouns* not on the list *to adjectives* of things that are. E.g., from truth to true thoughts, from science to true thoughts, etc. This aside is to warn you against claims that there are various types of truth. Some psychoanalysts, afraid truth will cause psychic harm to ~~patients,~~ ~~clients~~, consumers— officialese for persons changes so fast these days!— describe delusions as "therapeutic truth," scientists afraid there is no Truth describe their fictions as "pragmatically true," believers afraid of scientific truth describe their faith-hopes as "supernatural truths," believers who don't believe all thoughts come from the same divine source distinguish "revealed truth" from the rest, skeptics who fear no unprovable guess can be true use "historical truth" to mean "historians' constructed and revisionist mythologies," though we should use it as a synonym for what "true history" means here: true proposals <u>that</u> Descartes existed, <u>that</u> Descartes believed <u>that</u>... **End.**]

True, you see the green color 'of' an apple, feel 'its' smooth roundness, hear the crunch of your teeth into 'it,' taste 'its' tartness, and so on. That is, you experience the color, feel, sound, taste, etc., **but that's all!** If you try to prove there is an unripe apple, it will be in the future that you try and all you will get will be more (future!) colors, sounds, feels, tastes, and other sense-data. If apples hang out on trees, no one but God has ever seen one. Descartes was right to view in-side sensations as clues to the *possibility* that unsensed bodies—apples, trees, etc.—exist out-side. The physics of light, sound, and the nervous system (all 'verified' by sense-related clues) make that much clear and distinct. But clues to a *possibility* are not the same as guarantees of truth, as every juror must realize. Which is why Descartes introduced God's moral character—basically God's honesty—to validate his conviction that some of our ideas about bodies are true. Berkeley decided God had been telling Descartes the truth when God proposed to him the <u>possibility</u> that (unsensed) bodies do not exist. For Berkeley, our 'sensed world' is the only physical-body 'world' there is. Study Berkeley, Hume, and Kant to get clear and distinct on the virtual-reality 'world' idea. "The present state of our knowledge in physics is aptly characterized" is how Einstein praised the book from which this is (a copy of) one passage:

> Thus gradually philosophers and scientists arrived at the startling conclusion that since every object is simply the sum of its qualities, and since qualities exist only in the mind, the whole objective universe of matter and energy, atoms and stars, does not exist except as a construction of the consciousness. [...] As Berkeley, the archenemy of materialism, put it: "All the choir of heaven and furniture of earth, in a word all those bodies which compose the mighty frame of the world, have not any substance outside the mind... So long as they are not actually perceived by me, or do not exist in my mind, or that of any other created spirit, they must either have no existence at all, or else subsist in the mind of some Eternal Spirit." Einstein carried this train of logic to its ultimate limits by showing that even space and time are forms of intuition, which can no more be divorced from consciousness than can our concepts of color, shape, or size. Space has no objective reality except as an order or arrangment of the objects we perceive in it,

and time has no independent existence apart from the order of events by which we measure it. (L.Barnett, *The Universe and Dr. Einstein*, ch.2)

Such thinking, with a bit of adjusting here and there, is behind Einstein's question, reported in sentence one of A.Pais' *'Subtle is the Lord...'*: "Do you really believe the moon exists only if you look at it?" The TVFs you see, the sounds you hear, the pains and pleasures you feel, etc., won't change when you change from interpreting them as clues to unseen bodies to interpreting them as a non-documentary movie. You can think of the film clips you have seen of Kennedy's "Ich bin ein Berliner" speech either the way you normally do, as a *re-presentation* of real bodies in a real plaza, or the way (I trust) you think of Star Wars and Star Trek 'ships' and 'galaxies' as life-movie-*originals*. God is right now (re)offering you a choice.

Truth about others? How about us? "Us" can refer to all humans, including you. But it can also refer only to us out here beyond the perimeter of your experienced 'virtual-reality world.' [**Aside.** Are you one of those who do not like this emphasis on you, because you prefer us and we? "We" is the most dangerous of shorthands, because it is usually used to contrast us (all the same) to them (ditto). Every person is different. So different, in fact, that all are the same: unique. Why (do we) blame all Jews because many of them deserve the reproaches of Amos? And blame all Germans because so many (of them) did it? Why not praise all the Jews, because Amos, Jesus, and Marx were all Jews? And the Germans, because Bonhoeffer, von Moltke, Stauffenberg, et al, were all Germans? If the future is to be better than the past, then all individuals who—like Hegel and Marx (individuals)—subordinate us to a larger individual—state, class, blob, etc.—must imitate Descartes better and ask why they think anyone else exists. **End.**] Do any of us out here exist? You have come to the point where you've heard that maybe not even subatom-sized bodies exist, that unseen apples, unsensed hands lifting them to unfelt mouths, etc., are as fictitious as Santa, that 'apples,' 'hands,' etc., are mentally-coordinated sequences of shaped-colors and sounds, etc., the way the Dwarfs' cottage and Cinderella's slipper were. Your imagination, prompted by the movie-like sense-data, whips them into a 'world.' The only difference between your outside-a-theater and inside-a-theater experiences is this: you grew up never suspecting that it's not distant stars you see at night, whereas you are soon forgetful of the fact that those are only screen-colors and speaker-sounds, not a spaceship named Enterprise and the whoosh of its rocket engines. Apply: what you see as you 'read' along here is not a page of inked paper any more than a microfiche image of a page from the *New York Times* is. And, if you are Isaiah Berlin, it's not my voice you hear. What would God's voice be like?

Berkeley thought about persons in a way utterly different from the way he thought of apples, mouths, teeth, etc. He thought of persons as non-bodily things. Angel-persons enjoying private life-movies are not movies, though their 'bodies' are. Thoughts about them, he said, are notions, not ideas. [**Aside.** Here, the maxim, "Words connect directly, not with thoughts, but with the inner-model imagery," is crucial. Aim to create the right mini-model of Berkeley's inner-model to use when interpreting the meaning of his word-cues. **End.**] But, though he uses "idea" for bodies and "notion" for persons, he does not explore the question, "How can I know anything about **other** persons who are as unsensed as the materialists' 3-D bodies are?" What made him, if he existed, and what makes you, if you do, believe that **other** persons are any more real than unsensed bodies? Why do you think Berkeley ever existed? Why do you think I think he did? Why do you think I exist? What evidence do you have that any of the people mentioned in these pages ever existed? Or that any of the human bodies you believe in have any consciousness* attached to them as your body— if it exists—does? Perhaps your brain is connected to a computer feeding it spurious 'coded impulses' to deceive you. Maybe God created only one human person, you, and is systematically deceiving you. (*By the way, did you put "being awake" and "understanding the truth about what's going on" at the top of your "Prerequisites for being as completely happy as possible"?)

So, T, have you decided just what a person is yet? (You should be able to figure out whether you are the individual being addressed here. If you aren't T, don't feel you have to skip this paragraph. This is an open letter.) Start easy. Do you think large-scale bodies exist? That skin exists? That skin is colored? Do you think a man can be trapped in a woman's body? Your only justification for advocating Aquinas' apophatic view (we can say, not what God is, but what God is not) was "I can't create." You can't walk or talk, either, so does that mean you're not human? You have to make up your mind what "person" means when you say you are a person. I should have recommended M.Novak's *Belief and Unbelief* on the similarities between human and divine selves. Why?

I go back to the old Hebrew traditions. Read the *Genesis* story of creation. God is portrayed as knowing what the divine intention is. God does not say "Let there be light" and expect a big spider to appear. What appears is just what God intends, and God is perfectly pleased with the result. That is the main tradition in the west where "God" means a being who clothes the flowers of the fields, who knows the number of hairs on your head down to the very last one, who knows every thought you think. (God creates it—like this—and waits upon your response.) Do you doubt that I thought of each detail of this book? Or that you can think about each one? True, recent physicists and theologians have gone shopping in the east for an alternative, but what they've brought back is not a person-concept. Regardless of whether they call their import "God," "Gaia," "Mother (Nature, Earth, etc.)," "the One," "a Being Beyond Comprehension," or... ("Das Nichts"?) So, T, why don't you think God is a person? Don't fudge. Joseph Campbell didn't when he answered the priest-swimmer's "Do you believe in a personal God?" with "No, Father." He knew the difference, unless Sam Keen erred in reporting that Campbell travelled east, encountered the caste system in the flesh, and "returned a confirmed Westerner, celebrating the uniqueness of the person" (July '71 *Psychology Today*). The motto here is: A rows by any other name... Though only if it is repeated by someone who understands that neither rowses nor names exist.

STOP. Look around you right **now**. Listen carefully. Sniff. Taste. Notice what you feel that seems to be on your skin's out side. Attend to everything you feel that, it seems, is on your in side, starting with your scalp, your forehead muscles, your eye muscles, your nose, etc., right down to your fingers and toes. Take the quintalist point of view and realize that the only things you sense are the things you sense **now**: the TVF colors you see **now** (these!), the sounds you hear **now**, the... Apart from **this** TVF, **current** sounds, what you feel **now**, what else exists? First, whatever present memory-images you are aware of right **now**, and the very thought that is coming to you **now**. And, of course, you. Now, ask yourself: What else is there? **Is there anything else?** Re-read this paragraph (i.e., invite the source of your stream of consciousness to present you with similar TVFs, imagery, and the same thought), over and over, till you feel confident you've taken on a mind similar to the one which Descartes had while composing Meditations One and Six.

If he ever existed! Carl Rogers (if he did) once told R.Evans (if he did) that he agreed with Kant about there being "no reality except in terms of man's perception of it," and then rephrased his belief this way: "None of us knows for sure what constitutes objective reality and we live our whole lives in the reality as perceived." Why did he not show he meant it by adding: "I may even be talking to a phantom person"? Why did Kierkegaard (if he did) say that no individuals exist, since the Becoming-of-Being/NonBeing is the only reality, then complain that so many genuine Christians misunderstood and wrongly criticized him?! Why do you believe any of the people named in these *Re-Meditations* ever existed? I have made them all up, and even I don't exist. Only you do, and it's silly for you to keep thinking of any "we" or "us." There's only you. Imprisoned in your life-movie. Unable to take a peek at anything out on the other side of these colors you see (that are flush up against you), that is, unable to sneak a look at anything but your private stream of consciousness. You are alone, in the holodeck of your mind, adrift in the vast, endless nothingness of black space. If you don't believe that, then what alternative thoughts do you assent to? Thoughts alone can rocket you through the curtain of your sense-data.

[So, R, what is this work's **hugest claim**? Just this. Whatever claim you make about any of us and our thoughts is a **T**ruth claim. As such. Are those claims hubris, too? What basis do you have for your selectivity?]

Has God ever spoken to you? Prescientifically, we crave miracles. If a voice from a burning bush said "Take off your shoes, you're in God's presence," we'd believe. I hope I'd check for a hallucination. I still recall the only miracle—of love—that I ever experienced. Here is what I wrote in my diary that evening. Other people might not regard it as a miracle. They might know little about quantum-physics miracles, too.

> I suddenly felt the longing for a sign, if only of courtesy, if only for the sake of the woman I loved, who knelt in front of me, praying, I knew, for a sign... Suddenly Lord Marchmain moved his hand to his forehead; I thought he had felt the touch of the chrism and was wiping it away. "O God," I prayed, "don't let him do that." But there was no need for fear; the hand moved slowly down his breast, then to his shoulder, and Lord Marchmain made the sign of the cross. Then I knew that the sign I had asked for was not a little thing, not a passing nod of recognition, and a phrase came back to me from my childhood of the veil of the temple being rent from top to bottom.

Turing said that, in principle, you can't tell a purse'un from a masheen, even thuf **only purs'uns can learn rools, always obey them without exception, but freely brake them to proov the exception really iz won.** To prove his thesis, he built a computer to plan out this hole book. (I swear I'm not lying: a masheen wrote this). He even programmed his computer to 'sum up' the case argued for in these *Re-Meditations*. Be careful, though. Unless you read it critically and isolate the errors he built into the summayshun, you may get taken in and believe in Yahweh. Or, God forbid, in Allah! Take my word: you're alone. I swear (and I'm God): there's no one else out here. P.S. Don't let anyone tell you the above was from Charles Ryder's diary. Run the Berlin Test: whose voice does it sound like? His or mine?

Summation. Which scientific facts would I zero in on to prove to you (you do exist, and you are not me!) that Descartes (of course he existed!) was right in believing that you'd better believe your creator has ways of leading you to certainty about what is true, because otherwise you'll never have any sound reason to feel sure of anything. (**Can you sift truth from error?** Here? In texts on physics, psychology, and theology? In the Warren Report?) I like James' way of ending his 1898 Ingersoll Lecture on immortality: no one can put a limit on what is possible. If the number of souls is constantly increasing, no one can prove that they are not all immortal. He repeated that with emphasis later on when he added that he meant personal immortality, that he meant there is no way to prove that every memory and feeling of this life will not be eternally preserved, that there is no way to prove that everyone will not be able, eternally, to say "I am the same personal being who in old times upon the earth had those experiences." Should he have added that there is also no way to prove that God did not create just you and give you all these illusory thoughts about people like Descartes and James? Or that there is no way to prove that God has not created 5.7B people and made all of them think they have lived exactly the life you have lived up till now? That would mean that you are not alone, we are out here, but we all think we are whoever you think you are. Scientific proofs? Try these. You can remember them with this formula: bows, books, and brains.

First, **bows**. Rainbows. Rainbows name colors. Colors are powerful evidence for God. Colors, if they exist, are distinct from colorless bodies. Become as attentive as you possibly can to every experience when it seems that colors undeniably exist: e.g., when you get up in the dark of night and watch to see if the glorious dawn from on high breaks upon you, when you look up later at noonday to see if the cloudless sky is blue, when you examine diamonds or lead crystal under an intense beam of light, when you let a researcher inject the back of your brain with tiny jolts of color-less electricity, when you're under the covers at night and press gently against closed eyelids, etc. Decide: are you aware of colorless subatoms frisking in your dark skull, or bodyless TVF-colors as such? Beware of the "I see X but it doesn't appear like X because it appears like Y" non-sense subterfuge: it's analogous to "I see Santa who appears like Daddy most of the year," 100% the opposite of "I see Daddy under the mistletoe but he appears like Santa."

Next, **books.** This one. We 'feel' that the spatial orientation of our own body and that of bodies such as books are independent of each other. Kant denied that, since all are part of one sensed 'world.' Test his thesis. First, turn this 'book' upside down: the paragraph that was above this line is now below it. **Notice the change!** Your reading slows up enormously*. Second, stand on your head. Now, with both book and you upside down, you can read as easily as before. If the real world has the Arctic on top, you jut out at an angle. If the Aussies are down under and your up is really up, they're upside down. If Europe's maps are wrong, they're right side up and you've been reading upside down all your life! What a difference it makes, when you're driving, which way you hold the map. How much easier it is to direct people to a destination in front of you than behind you. This roomy 'world' is your private, **truly** real, sense-data 'world,' misleadingly called "**virtually** real." (*The addition problem in the center of the IMD has a new answer.)

Finally, **brains.** J.Harrison wants me to tell you that, since you were a month old, your omni-projector brain has been living in a laboratory tank, attached to me. I'm Hal, a supercomputer assigned to feed it nerve impulses the way your body's senses would have if they hadn't had to cut away your body (your brain's taxi) to keep you from an early demise. I have been enjoying my task of designing your 'world' and all the unreal characters in your life-story-line. **You know none of the real people out here, and none of the unreal people you believe in exist...** Oops, I'm getting a feedback signal that this tape is nearing the end. Ask for whatever program you want next, and if it's reasonable—within what I've decreed are the 'laws of nature'—I'll play it for you. In case you'd like to review the argument, tell me. How? Just will to turn back (go ahead?) to "Preface." What you see will be new, but it will look almost exactly like what you saw earlier. Though you'll have to rely on me to supply you later with true, not false, future thoughts about what you saw earlier.

Last words? Whose last words would they be? By the way, ask Turnig if computer-masheens can play this game of non-chess. And ask him, When is checkmate?

POST SCRIPT

If you meditate on the *Re-Meditations* outlook only one time, it will probably recede so far to the backroads of your mind that you may have difficulty recalling it. Only repetition can make it familiar enough to exert a powerful effect on your life. Please, though, do not take lightly the challenge to try on this new outlook by learning it well. Given the precarious situation of our planet as we approach a new millennium, you would not be wrong to regard the challenge as a moral obligation.

What is our precarious situation? Just this. Two possible futures loom ahead of us, one utopian, the other hellish. The latter is the one easiest for six o'clock news watchers to think of. Each evening we are treated to graphic scenes of murder and mayhem on a grand scale. The massive-scale is important. Nightly reports of single crimes in widely scattered areas add up in our minds to whole cities being slowly destroyed by urban warfare. Nightly reports of the struggles between rich and poor, majorities and minorities, minorities and minorities, add up in our minds to an entire nation being torn apart by cultural warfare. Nightly reports of armed conflicts in various regions of the world add up in our minds to an entire planet slowly succumbing to world-wide warfare. The 8-28-95 *Time* magazine highlights the result with its cover-story on modern society's state of increased depression and anxiety. Like Marx, it traces the state of society to economics. Better technology, the fruit of better science, has constantly made our life easier, richer, and longer, yet a consuming desire for More! makes us constantly aim to get ahead of where we are, no matter how far we've come. The emphasis on our happiness, not theirs, on our betterment, not theirs, and on our rights, not theirs, coupled with the emphasis on how their greed, their power, and their insensitivity are the barriers preventing us from achieving our happiness, our betterment, and our rights, fuels the conflicts which may, conceivably, lead to our mutual destruction.

The general framework proposed here gives a radical twist to current political and economic debates. There are no groups, hence no governments, no forms of them, no corporations, no written human laws, no money, no apples, etc. There are, though, individual persons like you and me, each is a learner whose thought-habits consist of a commonsense core overlaid with a cultural veneer. Capitalism, socialism, hinduism, buddhism, judeao-christianity, islam, etc., are cues for cultural-veneer, thought-habit veils which must be drawn aside in order to see what's real: individuals with their individual enjoyments sought, efforts expended, pains endured, hopes held, worries carried, etc. The *Time* essay reported that not every group feels depression and anxiety as extensively as every other, that—for instance—Old Order Amish suffer from depression "at less than one-fifth the rate of people in nearby Baltimore." The question is why.

At the beginning of this century, James published two series of lectures in a book called *The Varieties of Religious Experience*. It is really a study in human nature, which is why he used that as its subtitle. But he might have called it Change of Habits or Conversion of Mores (an old name for habits). It is about the relation between belief- and life-habits on the one hand and optimism-vs-pessimism on the other. While still young, James had a crucial encounter with depression and was tempted to suicide, and he wrote that his sanity was saved only by clinging to such scripture texts as "God is my refuge," "I am the resurrection and the life," etc. From then on, the desire to find *sound reasons* to believe that our prayers are not addressed to a deaf universe was never far from his concerns. Careful study will show that this is the key to his most famous work, *Pragmatism*, and that he always coupled questions about God or the gods with his insistence on the value of moral striving. Unless we have hope that our efforts can achieve something valuable, not just for the moment, but for eternity, cosmic pessimism is the only rational stance to adopt. It is worth noting that Bertrand Russell supported James' argument. He opted for the deaf universe. In "A Free Man's Worship," he drew a picture of the world's final conflagration, then added: "...only on the firm foundation of despair, can the soul's habitation henceforth be safely built." Well, at this end of the century, praxis has demonstrated just how 'safe' is what can be built on a we-humans-are-alone-in-the-universe, despairing-of-the-*ultimate*-future foundation.

What remedy is there for *some* people's increasing depression and anxiety? Increased pay, better sex, no-side-effects pills, "defecating twice a day with unfailing regularity" (Russell's admitted source of happiness) may help. But death confronts us all. For you—the 6 o'clock news won't let you forget it—death may come sooner than you think. James was right. Only *knowing* we are in good hands, etc...